A Twist in the 1

By Phil Maddock

A Twist in the Tail

Snoring and oinking loudly, the youngest and smartest of the three pigs turned in his sleep, scuffling the sheet down past his trotters onto the dusty floor. It was a hot, sticky evening and the tired pig had not slept well. In and out of sleep all night, he had been battling against the discomfort of his bed and his airless room, as well as his mother's incessant partying downstairs. It was the same almost every night; music, visitors, shouting and other related noises. Davey was fed up of it. He was a lively and intelligent little pig who communicated well with his brothers and the other farm animals. This had made him a popular choice when the quarterly farm quiz came round and animals would spend weeks in the build up to the quizzes trying to convince him to be on their team. He'd had enough of being kept awake all night though and it was time for him to do something about it; time to make some changes. Grumpy and frowning, he pushed himself up and twisted round on the bed, planting his feet on the thin blanket of straw that lay scattered about the bedroom floor. He sat there, hunched and miserable. Looking up, he noticed that Harvey, his eldest brother by a matter of minutes, was stirring in his bed. Harvey wasn't what you would call an academic and had always performed badly at Farm School; that was when Cynthia, their mother, had had enough concern for them to make sure they went to school. Harvey was, however, an excellent cook. He'd spent most of his childhood staring into the kitchen of the farmhouse, watching the farm chef expertly preparing all the meals for the busy farmworkers.

As if sensing that his younger brother was awake, Harvey continued shuffling and eventually opened his eyes to look straight at Davey. Immediately, he could see that there was something not quite right; they had found themselves in this position many times but on this night, Davey had a different expression on his face. It was one of defeat, anxiety and frustration. Harvey threw Davey a sympathetic look and stood up to go to the toilet, sighing heavily with relief once he got there. By the time he returned, Davey was scribbling on a piece of paper.

"What you doing?" Harvey asked.

"I'm done." Davey replied. "I'm writing a note to mum to tell her that I'm leaving. Or that we're leaving. Up to you."

"You can't leave. Mum needs us. Who will keep the sty safe? And where on Earth are you gonna go?"

"I can't stay here, Harvey, mate. We're wasting our lives here. Let's wake Stan up and see what he says."

Stanley's bed was in the far corner of the room and, for a while now, he had been stirring from a half decent sleep. He was the fittest and strongest of the three pigs. A fine specimen of a creature; athletic, brave and courageous. He had heard everything that the two brothers had been talking about.

"Let's go." he said, rubbing his eyes. "I've had enough of this place. Mum doesn't care. She's only interested in having a good time. All we do is clear up the mess she leaves behind; it's depressing. God knows what she's up to half the time. She needs help. I'm with Davey."

The three brothers stood facing each other. It was 3:26am. As the party began to die down and the revellers began to make their way home, the young pigs began to concoct a plan of escape... and, more importantly, a plan of action.

Cynthia, a bottle of beer in hand and a half smoked cigarette hanging loosely from her mouth, trudged loudly upstairs. She never made any attempts to not disturb her sleeping children; so regularly did she throw her famous parties, it had become common practice for her to trip over her own trotters on her way upstairs, or knock something over in the hallway, or even stagger accidentally into the wrong room and collapse onto one the three pigs' own beds, with them still barely sleeping under the covers. On this occasion however, Cynthia reached the top of the stairs and managed to weave her way gracefully along the hallway to her own bedroom. Fiddling with the door handle only briefly, she swung her door open, carefully closed it with a loud bang and fell in a heap on her unmade bed. Even if she had tripped and fallen onto Stanley's, Harvey's or Davey's bed, due to her intoxication, it was unlikely that she would have realised that the beds were empty. That her children were gone. And that they were not coming back. Not for a while at least.

By the time the party had finished and Cynthia had managed to find her way to her bedroom, the three pigs had agreed on a plan and finalised their note. They gathered the things they thought they were going to need and were now huddled in the corner of the garage at the entrance of the farm, behind a red tractor that belonged to farmer George. It was 5:15am and the sun was beginning to rise, creating a soft, golden blanket that seemed to cover everything that could be seen across the landscape. A few of the other farm animals had begun to stir; at least those who did not attend Cynthia's party and had woken with the sunrise, full of morning energy. Claire, the horse in the field behind the pigsty, was strolling around her meadow and had sensed some movement coming from the entrance of the farm. She stood still, her long face drooping over the fence, staring at the farm's main gate. She was good friends with Davey and his brothers and for a long time had been concerned for their well-being as she was well aware of the goings on in their home. On many occasions, Claire and Cynthia had had heated arguments about various things; how tired the pigs looked or how late the noise had lasted at a recent party. Claire had taken it upon herself to look after and care for the three pigs whenever they were out of their barn. She allowed them to snooze in her warm and comfortable stable during the day and regularly provided them with fresh food and leftovers. Cynthia called her an interfering cow, which Claire always found amusing, seeing as she was a horse. Agitated at the disturbance she had noticed, Claire became restless and began trotting anxiously up and down the length of her field.

Surveying the farm through a crack in the wall of the garage, Stanley spotted Claire and immediately felt a stab of guilt in his gut.

"We should go and tell her what we're doing." he whispered to his brothers. "She'll be worried sick if we disappear without a trace.

"OK. But don't let anyone see you." said Davey. "If Farmer George or any of the other animals hear anything, we'll be found out and we'll never be able to escape once he sets up round the clock surveillance."

Stanley skulked across the farm, watching in all directions for any movements coming from different corners and shadows around the grange. George was still asleep - his bedroom window dark and the curtains drawn. Some of the chickens were strutting around their coop but fortunately for the three pigs, Johnny, the farm's Cock, had been one of the last to leave Cynthia's party and he was dead to the world, snoring noisily. The last thing Stanley wanted was Johnny cock-a-doodle-doing at the top of his voice, waking everyone on the farm. Billy the Goat, who's field Stanley had to navigate before reaching Claire's meadow, stood sleeping, still as a statue; another attendee at the soiree the night *before.*

From the corner of her eye, Claire noticed Stanley trying to get her attention at a narrow gap in the tall hedge of her field. She hadn't seen him moving through the farm, such was the expert way in which he'd managed to keep himself out of sight. She turned and galloped urgently over to where he was. He explained to her what was going on and what he and his brothers were up to, but told her very little detail of the actual plan they had devised. At first she refused to let them go, threatening to neigh at the top of her voice to wake up the farm. But she also knew that this was something the three pigs had to do. For themselves, by themselves. She promised that she would do her best to look after their mother in their absence and she insisted that the three pigs stay in touch. She requested that Stanley allow her to speak to Henry, the carrier pigeon, reassuring him that Henry was trustworthy and professional and had a proven track record, with a string of outstanding testimonials to his name; he would make sure that Claire was kept reliably informed of how the piglets were getting on.

Claire tried not to get too emotional when it came to say goodbye and Stanley, young and naïve as he was, also found himself with a lump in his throat. He made it back to the Farmhouse without incident and he could see Davey and Harvey crouching behind the wheel of the tractor. Harvey was gesticulating furiously in Stanley's direction, waving his trotter in the air as if to tell Stanley not to come any closer. Stanley froze. He was stood against the Farmhouse wall and could see the extensive driveway and the large sturdy gates that were never shut, due to the pleasant nature of the people in the local community. Before he had seen Harvey's protestations at his advancing, Stanley was about to stealth his way towards the tractor, to the left of the main gates. It would have meant that he would have had to be exposed for a short while between the front of the Farmhouse and the safety of the tractor and the garage in which it was parked. Still frozen, Stanley scanned the area from his covert position and ...

Ron. A loyal, well-mannered Golden Retriever, with a good nose and a playful personality. Ron made a great farm dog. He got on well with all the animals and played nicely with Farmer George's children. He provided a sympathetic ear to the senior animals when they wanted to talk about problems on the farm or with their friends or families; he frolicked with the younger animals and kept them safe when visitors came driving too quickly into the farmyard in their delivery vans; he even resolved disputes between the farm animals during times of disagreement and unrest by acting as a mediator when things got ugly. Most important of all were Ron's guarding attributes. Eager, alert and energetic, Ron was always busy, always sniffing around and looking about. Stanley knew that the minute Ron saw the three pigs out of the barn on their own, he would alert the farmer and they'd be returned swiftly to their unsuspecting mother. Stanley slipped out of sight of the watchful dog who was circling around the driveway with his nose to the ground and his tail wagging in the air.

A gust of wind swirled around the farm, picking leaves off the fields and churning them around in spiral patterns. All of a sudden, the whistling howl of the morning wind died down and a silence fell about the farm. Ron stopped in his tracks. Stanley held his breath. Harvey and Davey looked on, wide-eyed from beneath the tractor, hidden mainly by the large muddied tyres. Ron's head lifted up and they could see him sniffing the air curiously. He moved a step and turned slightly to his left, sniffing again, his right front leg hovering in the air. Another faint breeze picked up through the farm and Ron caught a whiff of something coming from the back of the Farmhouse. He couldn't quite put his finger on it. Perhaps a window was open; perhaps the cook was already preparing the day's nutrition. Surely he wouldn't be working already at this hour. Could it be a scent drifting across from a nearby farm? Ron traversed the driveway in search for a better idea of the scent he had caught, zigzagging towards the location of Harvey and Davey in the garage. They didn't dare move a muscle. Stanley looked on anxiously, his left leg sliding slowly out in front of him as he hugged the corner wall of the Farmhouse, ready to create a diversion of some kind.

Just then, the door of the Farmhouse opened and a sleepy-looking Mary poked her head out. Mary was George's wife and had grown up around animals all her life. She was an expert at picking out the best stock at any of the local animal auctions and she had also had a major say in the new layout of Hillside Farm when she and George had decided to focus more on organically grown produce. Mary called for Ron and turned to walk inside. Ron, his interest in the intriguing scent in the air vanishing as soon as he knew breakfast was waiting for him, did a one-eighty and dashed inside, hurtling past Mary into the kitchen. Stanley and his brothers sighed simultaneously as the door closed and gathered once more in the safety of the garage behind the tractor. Stanley gave his brothers a steely look of determination, as if to suggest that this might not be the last close call they would encounter over the course of their journey.

A calming stillness settled upon the Hillside Farm. Only the early birds could be heard clearing their throats and beginning to warm up their vocal chords with intermittent and irregular birdsongs. Perhaps there were too few other birds awake to respond. There was, however, one bird who was wide awake. One bird who had spent the last few minutes trying to reassure a frantic Claire that he would watch over the piglets once they'd left the farm. Henry sat alone in the tallest tree on the farm, an old and magnificent oak tree which sat at the rear of the farm, overlooking the entire countryside. It was from here that Henry surveyed the whole area and as the Spring-morning sun continued to rise, the oak tree's long shadow stretched out across Claire's field below it. The oak tree grew out of the pathway that weaved through the farm, right from the main gate, all the way to the rear. It stood in between Claire's field and Billy the Goat's patch of grass. Next to Billy lived Johnny, all alone at the moment, while George and Mary were searching for a new batch of hens. There were various other fields and animals that made up the busy little farm, the mud pit being the longest-standing feature.

The three pigs loved to play noisily in that mud pit and it was certainly the thing that they would miss most while they were gone.

Silently, they slipped out of the garage, through the main gates of the farm and onto the road for the very first time. They stayed out of sight in the hedgerows as much as possible. The early morning traffic amounted to nothing more than the occasional milk float, but the little pigs did not want to take anything for granted. Navigating the thorny brambles and thick bush, they sometimes had to nip out into the road and dash along to the next section of hedge that was possible to get through. Henry, the carrier pigeon, flew unnoticed, landing at various look out points along the way and he maintained a watchful eye over the journeymen as he went. Claire was right; Henry was vigilant and adept.

A bit of background information before we continue

Prior to the birth of Harvey and his younger brothers, their mother, Cynthia, was a healthy and happy gilt. Her partner, Jeremy, was a large, powerful boar and they were both very much in love. Life on Hillside Farm was idyllic; eating leftovers, relaxing in the mud pools, sleeping heavily and socialising with the other animals regularly. When the piglets were born, Cynthia's relationship with Jeremy became strained. Although there was a school on the farm for the younger animals, there were no marriage guidance groups or new parent support groups. As a relatively young couple based on a farm to which they had recently been introduced, they were left to work things out for themselves. Even though they both loved their children, and each other, perhaps they weren't quite prepared for the challenges and difficulties they would have to face. The stresses of rearing three lively piglets, combined with the sleep deprivation associated with parenthood, became all too much for them. They began to argue over every decision and quarrel during every meal. And the amount of time they spent eating, meant that they argued pretty much most of the time. Slowly, the relationship began to deteriorate and the pair communicated less and grew further apart. Without the advice of a wise old boar or sow to rely on, they couldn't manage to support one another in the same way they once did.

As the months rolled on, The Wolf, a shady and unlikeable character who was always on the lookout for vulnerable specimens such as Cynthia, would make increasingly regular trips to the farm to deliver whatever he thought she needed. The Wolf was a crafty and manipulative beast who had taken a recent interest in this particular little farm. He had watched the animals and learned their habits and movements. That way, he was able to sneak onto the farm unnoticed whenever he felt like it, but mainly at nightfall. He had convinced Cynthia that he would be able to help her. In return, all he asked was his picking from their healthy pile of food scraps. She thought this was a fair deal, particularly if it helped to improve how she was feeling. What she didn't know was that Wolf always had a second agenda; he hoped to gain the trust of Cynthia so that when the time was right, when her little pigs were fat enough, he would be able swipe them away from Hillside Farm right under her nose and she wouldn't even notice a thing. Yes, he could have just eaten them all there and then but The Wolf was thinking of the long game and was prepared to wait for these special tasty morsels to grow. Also, so manipulative and cunning was he that he sickly enjoyed *this particular type of hunt. The Wolf always thought that a hunt such as this, one that took time and preparation, always brought about a more satisfying feast in the end. So Cynthia began taking sleeping pills and other barbiturates that she thought would help her cope. And she became reliant on a whole host of different 'vitamins and minerals', as The Wolf called them. Wolf saw it as a win – win situation; he could sneak onto the farm and help himself to the finest cuts of the leftovers that were fed to the pigs (George and Mary liked to take great care of all their animals and particularly with their new organic philosophy, their leftovers pile was the best out of all the farms in the area) and he could infiltrate and control a young family, with the intention of striking just at the right moment, just when they were least expecting it. He felt that after all the work he was going to put into the project, he would be fully deserving of an easy kill when the time came.*

Jeremy was unaware of these visits and couldn't understand Cynthia's erratic behaviour, blaming himself for the way things had turned out. Wolf's visits were always carefully planned and meticulously timed so that he rarely ran into anyone and always managed to get Cynthia when she was alone; wither just before bedtime when everyone else was already asleep, or early in the morning before anyone had risen. As time went on, it became increasingly easy for the Wolf to meet with Cynthia. In fact, it got to a point that she would actually ask him when he would be visiting next and what he would be bringing with him. Jeremy came to the conclusion that Cynthia's life as a sow would be better without him. One afternoon, during a rare civil conversation between the two, Jeremy and Cynthia decided that it would be the best for everyone if they separated, or at least spent some time apart. Cynthia, at the time, was susceptible to any suggestion and more occupied with thoughts of when The Wolf would be making his next run. Jeremy put in place his plan of action; he needed to get away from the farm but a beast his size couldn't just walk out through the gates unnoticed. He feigned illness and began walking around the farm with a worsening limp, to suggest that there was something wrong with his foot. He also began dribbling occasionally from his mouth to really give George something to think about. The farmer became concerned and took him to the vet to be checked over.

It was during this visit that Jeremy escaped to the mountains to live alone. During one evening when the members of the veterinary clinic were asleep, he managed to quietly dismantle the planks of the wooden door to his temporary sty and flee into the night. He became a recluse and learnt to live off the land, adapting to the harsh environments and challenges that were presented to him on a daily basis. Jeremy became a folk story that animals would retell to their friends and families over supper. Animals on the various farms throughout the countryside would eavesdrop on their human owners during dinnertime and listen as they talked about strange sightings and abnormal noises coming from the hills. As time passed, stories changed from tales of a mystical nomad roaming the *mountaintops, to rumours of a crazy, deformed figure, hiding away in the shadows. The three piglets knew very little of their father but judging from the accounts told to them by other animals on the farm, he was a loyal and caring father who doted on his sons before the split. Jeremy had done his best to support his family but it seemed that he and Cynthia just couldn't see eye to eye and lacked the communication skills to explain this to each other. As she became more reliant on her pills, she became more difficult to reach and Jeremy, being a simple pig, simply couldn't understand why things had turned out the way they had. The three of them had always wanted to find him and help their parents rekindle the love that was once so strong.*

This was the first part of their plan. They had only a vague idea of where their father might be and even less idea of what sort of pig he had now become. Were any of the stories even close to the truth? Would they recognise him if and when they found him? Would he even remember or acknowledge them? These were questions that the three brothers had not discussed with each other, but all of them had considered personally, during the countless hours lying awake at night.

All the animals of Hillside Farm knew of The Wolf. At pyjama parties and sleepovers, the younger animals would tell tales of The Wolf's violence and destruction. Most of these stories were made up – a game of who could come up with the scariest versions, but eventually, truth and myth became entwined and now, nobody knew where The Wolf was or if he would reappear.

ever he visited Cynthia at the Farm, he would do so
ticed, quietly making his way to the pigsty to deliver
his goods. Even though the creatures of Hillside Farm
were aware of The Wolf's existence, they knew nothing
about his regular attendance.

Little did they know, ~~he was~~ regularly
of his secret visits to the farm.

The beginning of the twirly tale

The journey into the mountains was arduous and fraught with possible dangers. Three naive little pigs out in the wilderness on their own would be easy and tasty pickings for any hungry predators waiting in the dark; or, for that matter, waiting behind a little bush in broad daylight. The young trio lacked any real experience of survival in the great outdoors, although Davey had always thrived at Farm School and was already helping his brothers to prepare of the adventure ahead. He was full of helpful hints about finding water that was safe to drink and rubbing themselves with mud to hide their scent. Being pigs, they had absolutely no trouble at all in excelling at the latter and maintained a sufficient coat of mud at all times, writhing enthusiastically in any mud pit they came across. In the little time they had to prepare, Davey had packed some survival satchels that each of them had draped tightly over their shoulders and secured firmly under their little bellies. Contained within these satchels, among other things, were some water bags, complete with straws, a few parcels of pig feed and a selection of leftover fruits and vegetables that Harvey had rustled up the night before. Stanley also chipped in with some ideas about moving as a group, staying together and communicating silently at times of expected peril.

According to Davey's calculations, it would take them approximately three days to traverse the awkward terrain and make it to the vicinity, in which it was believed, that Jeremy was last seen. Within just a few hours of setting off, the determined pigs found themselves at the base of Wakeman's Hill, a small but steep gradient that folklore had revealed, was where Jeremy had spent his first few nights after escaping from the veterinary clinic. A picturesque setting stood before them; dainty waterfalls and pretty flowers created a calming and pleasurable atmosphere for the little would-be heroes. They admired the beautiful scene surrounding them and drank thirstily from their water bags, refilling them from the quaint streams as they went. Briefly, their mission was forgotten and the pigs talked jovially of good times on the farm, as they followed the walkway that had been created over the years by continuous trampling. The sun sat high in the sky and shone brightly down on the piglets. It was hot and tiresome work but what with Davey's helpful hints, Stanley's awful jokes and Harvey's reminiscing, they were all relishing their first day out from Hillside Farm. They were making steady progress and were approximately three quarters of the way up Walkman's Hill when all of a sudden,

Stanley's right trotter, tightly clenched in a fist, shot up over his shoulder. The pigs crouched and froze. Even though they had momentarily lost concentration, they were surprisingly quick to react to Stanley's command. Stanley surveyed the area. A rustling up ahead could be heard and Stanley, peeking from behind an elevated rock, spotted some movement – only a quick glimpse but definitely a disturbance of some kind. He slowly glanced back over his shoulder, indicating to his brothers to remain still while he ventured forward to investigate.

The brave little pig moved with utmost care. He was very deliberate with every step he took and made sure to move any over hanging branches out of his way as he went, so as not to create any unnecessary movements that would give away his position. Stooping low through where the undergrowth prevented him to stand, and darting skilfully from hiding places to shadowy areas, Stanley sustained his steady advance towards his target - the point at which he saw the disturbance in the shrubberies. A deftly performed forward roll to the base of a tree was Stanley's penultimate move before gaining the vantage point he sought. The climbing of the willow tree would be his next. With a strong leap, Stanley pulled himself up onto the first branch and squeezed himself up and through the entangled arms of the tree. It wasn't a very tall tree but Stanley was extremely well hidden in its thick foliage. When he reached the highest point of the tree, he scanned the area once more and... he saw it. Or rather them; he saw them. A skulk of foxes lazing in the darks among the bushes. All five of them, a fine Reynard, a beautiful vixen and three healthy cubs, were resting in *the exact point the three pigs had to go through to get to their next checkpoint. A little piglet would be a welcome meal for a family of foxes. Three small pigs would make for a memorable banquet – one that even a certain fantastic fox would be proud of. Stanley scrambled through to the other side of the tree and managed to get the attention of Davey who was always alert, particularly at times of danger. Stanley indicated some instructions to Davey and the three met in a huddle at the bottom of the tree.*

After much deliberation and heated debate, they agreed on what they were to do next. Due to the formations of the mountainside, there was no way around that particular section. Large rocks jutted high out of the ground either side, making it impossible to veer from the path. The pigs were going to have to confront this problem or turn around and go home. Decisions are easy to make when you only have one option. They took up positions on the hill, below the snoozing foxes. They had already ascertained that the wind was blowing downhill, so there was no risk of their scent travelling up to the foxes' sensitive noses. Of course, their muddied bodies also protected them from this. Stanley closed in, just a few feet away from the group and nearest to the largest fox, the male. Harvey maintained his distance and fumbled with the large selection of acorns, cones and conkers that he held in the red neckerchief that he liked to wear around his neck when he prepared food. Davey was crouched and very still. He held a small mirror that he'd packed into his satchel and was experimenting with the reflection it created, trying to get his angles just right. He remembered times in Farm School when he was waiting for Daisy the cow to finish explaining a complicated topic to the class – Davey would already know the ins and outs of whatever she was clarifying and he would deflect the rays of sun from the face of his watch, directing them into the eyes of his fellow students. Some of them would look across immediately at where the flicker of light came from, by which time Davey was sat upright in his seat, seemingly engrossed in what Daisy was saying. He never got caught, not once. This however was a totally different situation. He was careful not to point the sunbeam towards the foxes just yet.

[handwritten annotation: Already knowing and bored]

[handwritten annotation: Intelligent and bored]

Slowly, Stanley edged closer still. He could almost reach out and grab the ears of the large fox in front of him. He clasped a rock in both hands that he'd unearthed from near the willow tree. The piglets glanced across at each other and each of them seemed to take a deep breath before simultaneously leaping into action. Davey aimed the mirror directly into the eyes of the larger male fox, blinding him completely. He squinted and grimaced at the uncomfortable interruption to his snooze. The light beam was so powerful that even through closed eyelids, the fox sensed the brightness. This made him open his eyes and he was immediately bedazzled. Meanwhile, Harvey frantically threw his ammunition at the group, pelting the vixen and the three cubs with proficient targeting. The leash of foxes had been awoken from their slumber by an unexpected chain of events; their father had been blinded by a strange bright light and the rest of them had been rained upon *with hard nuts from what seemed to be all sides. Pandemonium ensued and as soon as the father tried to stand, Stanley leapt high into the air, holding the rock above his head. The scream he let out ripped through the hillside, making the already jumpy and under-fire group, jolt again with further fright. The rock came crashing down on the skull of the fox, rendering it unconscious. Stanley stood in the centre of the circle of frightened foxes, wide-eyed, breathing heavily. His brothers bounded into the circle and the three of them held their arms aloft in triumph, oinking loudly. The four remaining foxes scarpered in all directions without hesitation, leaving their comatose father at the mercy of these apparently deranged and dangerous pigs.*

"We don't want to be around when he wakes up." *Harvey said, kneeling down at the head of the wounded fox, who was motionless apart from the slight raising and lowering of his side, indicating that there was still life in the old dog yet. A flutter in the leaves above startled the trio for a moment and they saw a pigeon flap out of the treetops and fly away in the direction of Hillside Farm. Stanley explained to his brothers that Claire had insisted upon hiring the services of Henry, a carrier pigeon. Harvey and Davey glanced at each other with a concerned look on their faces. They didn't like the idea that they had been followed the whole day without even realising it.*

"Don't worry." *Stanley reassured them.* *"He's only keeping Claire informed about how we are getting on. She wouldn't have let us leave the farm if I didn't agree*

to it. And besides, when mum finds our note, Claire's going to need to tell her that we're OK."

They were all agreed that Cynthia would need to be told that her children were alive. Despite her debauched lifestyle, she was still their mother. Without time for further contemplation, the pigs moved silently into the shadows of the canopied woodland again. They seemed to be moving through the coppice with more confidence in their strut. They were looking around far less frequently and operating as a more organised group. Occasionally, Stanley would dart ahead or veer off to the left or right, checking for footprints or sniffing out for scents of any kind. Davey and Harvey would either spread out to get a better view of their surroundings, or walk shoulder to shoulder, protecting one another's blindside. For the most part of their advancing however, the group would move in single file through the undergrowth, leaving as little disturbance behind them as possible and creating as little noise or disruption as they could. It seemed that the Three Little Pigs were learning fast that in order to survive this adventure, they would need to be instinctive and decisive, and they would need to trust each other, absolutely.

They continued like this until nightfall, by which time they reached the top of Wakeman's Hill and located a suitable place to set up camp. Well, to say set up camp would be an overstatement. They each found a secluded little nook and fell asleep, resting their weary heads on their satchels.

Cynthia rouses...

Meanwhile, back at Hillside Farm, Cynthia was just beginning to stir from her drunken collapse. She was bleary eyed and her head hurt. Immediately reaching for her cigarettes, she lit up and inhaled deeply, not particularly enjoying it but smoking it nonetheless. Contrary to what one might think of a depressed and intoxicated sow, Cynthia took personal hygiene extremely seriously. She showered, flossed and brushed her teeth and applied a little too much foundation to her chops, before getting ready to spend the rest of her day in the mud pool. Covering her eyes as she left her sty, in preparation for the powerful glare of the afternoon sun, Cynthia stopped and looked around, bewildered. She lowered her trotters. There was no need to cover her eyes. It wasn't the afternoon; it was late in the evening. Cynthia had slept right through the day and hadn't stirred. Again. This always made her feel even more depressed than usual because she felt that she had *missed the day – she'd certainly missed an opportunity to relax in the mud. But more than that, it made her feel worthless and hollow. And it was part of the endless, vicious cycle she found herself in. The only thing to do now, she thought to herself, was to turn around, have a drink and hope for the arrival of The Wolf. Upon turning, she noticed something at the entrance of the pigsty. A small piece of folded paper – Cynthia picked it up, wondering how she hadn't seen it on her way outside. Squinting, as if that might ease the pain in her head and help her to see better, she unfolded the paper and tried to focus on it.*

Dear Mum,

We love you. But we cannot stay at home anymore. You don't look after us and you spend too much time with animals we don't like. You stay up too late and because of the noise that's made at your parties, we don't get enough sleep. We have gone to look for Dad. Maybe he will know what to do. We have gone to ask him why he left us. We think you are not well and we want you to get better because we know that you're a good person and that you love us. We don't know when we will return. Perhaps when we are older, we can look after you.

Love from

Harvey, Stanley and Davey.

Xxx

Cynthia crumpled up the note in her fist and clenched it tight. She steadied herself against the wall as the contents of the letter began to sink in. She had failed her children. She had failed as a mother and a sow. Cynthia began to sob uncontrollably, falling in a heap on the floor. She reached up and grabbed the only thing that had helped her through times of hardship and pain. The bottle. The note tumbled from her trotters as she grasped the bottle with both hands and raised it shakily to her mouth. The bottle was tilted to an almost vertical position and bubbles ran up the inside of the glass, replacing the liquid that poured into Cynthia's eager mouth. Bringing the bottle down to her side, Cynthia's cheeks bulged with the amount of fluid she had tipped into herself. Then, in a fit of rage, she spat it out, spraying the drink across the room, her face reddened with despair and soaked with sweat. She stood up unsteadily and threw the bottle against the wall, smashing it violently into hundreds of jagged pieces. It left a huge wet stain where it smashed and shards of glass scattered through the air, landing everywhere. In the middle of the room she stood, panting heavily. She had just thrown away her dearest possession; the thing she turned to when she was feeling down. It was the best friend she had in this world and Cynthia had obliterated it where she stood. Collapsing again, she picked up the note and read it three, maybe four more times, sobbing all the while.

Just then, Claire walked in. She'd sprinted across the

farm when she heard the loud crash and the subsequent sobbing.

"Cynthia!" she exclaimed, rushing up to her traumatised friend. "What's going on?"

She dropped to her knees and comforted Cynthia immediately. Even though they had their differences, Claire and Cynthia had known each other for a long time and deep down, they cared for one another greatly. The two of them lay there for ages. Of course, Claire knew exactly 'what was going on', but to relay that now to Cynthia would just upset her even further. Eventually, Cynthia was able to talk and the pair spoke in great depth about recent events and how things had turned out the way they had. Cynthia listened intently as Claire relayed to her the information Henry had provided during his reconnaissance mission of the piglets' quest - where the pigs had journeyed, how brave they were being and what they mostly likely planned to do next. It wasn't until sunrise that Claire realised just how drained Cynthia looked. It upset Cynthia deeply that her little piglets had turned to Claire for help and support, rather than their own mother. She understood why and she didn't blame Claire for this, it just made her feel all the more terrible about what impact her lifestyle had had on her children. Claire took her friend upstairs and tucked her in, returning downstairs to make something for her to eat when she awoke. She also considered tidying up, thinking to herself that the place looked like a pigsty.

First light the next morning

A few miles northwest of Hillside Farm, a loud rumbling woke Harvey from his sleep. At first, he couldn't make out where it was coming from, but he soon realised by how hungry he felt that it was the sound from his own belly, reverberating around the little alcove he had found himself. It wasn't just Harvey who'd heard the noise and he wasn't alone in waking up feeling peckish. The Three Pigs congregated drowsily in the clearing, on the outskirts of which they had all spent the night. Groggy but determined, they snacked on the fruits and vegetables from within their satchels. Harvey, proud of the perfect amount of seasoning he had applied, commented on each mouthful and encouraged his brothers to give him some critical feedback about what they thought of his dish. They both stated that the food bits were indeed delicious, but perhaps now wasn't the time to dwell on Harvey's culinary successes or failures. After a short drink, the pigs set off once again. They had conquered Wakeman's Hill and expertly ambushed and dissembled a group of foxes that would normally have eaten three juicy piglets for breakfast, lunch and dinner. They found no sign of their father's presence in the area; it was four years since he left and any trace of him would surely have been washed away by now.

Through large patchwork fields and rolling hilltops, the little porkers trekked and trekked hard. Remaining out of sight in tall grasses and keeping in the shaded areas as much as possible, Davey and his brothers were in an almost buoyant mood. And they had every right to be; the odds were stacked against them getting even this far. Stanley spoke about how well he'd slept the night before, even though it was his first night away from the farm. Harvey reiterated the fact that the seasoning on his veggies had been just right and that he was looking forward to doing a bit of scavenging along the walk. Every now and then, a disturbance of some kind would frighten them; a stark reminder that they were still vulnerable out in the wilderness. On occasion, they would spot Henry swooping high in the sky, or flapping in the branches of the tallest trees. The carrier pigeon had returned to Claire twice since the pigs had left and she was becoming more and more intrigued about the purpose of their venture. She'd given Henry instructions to interfere as little as possible with the little piglets but to do his best to keep them safe.

By early afternoon, the back of the second day's trek was broken and the three pigs stumbled wearily towards the incline of Seeker's Peaks, a much larger and more

*treacherous duo of mountain tops than Wakeman's Hill.
As the hours of the day had passed, the weather had
become a little more turbulent and the grasses danced
more vigorously in the breezes. Looking about him,
Harvey noticed the clouds were growing darker and
seemed to be closer to them now. He wasn't sure if it
was to do with the fact that he was higher up, or
because the clouds were getting bigger and therefore
loomed more ominously in the sky. A stiff gust of wind
blew into his chops and caught him off guard. Stanley
placed a reassuring set of knuckles on Harvey's shoulder
and they soldiered onwards. As they continued to ascend
the dominating escarpment of Seeker's Peaks, the path
become narrow and rocky. It weaved its way up towards
the nearest ridge and disappeared over it, only coming
into view again further ahead, in the lead up to the
second, higher crest. A few droplets of rain began to fall
upon the heads and backs of the Three Pigs and for a
while, they were glad for the cooling sensation it
brought. However, it also made the ground more
slippery underfoot and as the rain grew heavier, it
became increasingly more difficult to make any real
headway. They battled along the footpath. Stanley
wondered to himself how such paths were formed –
despite the rocky nature of the path, it didn't look as
though someone had carefully laid down paving stones
and it wasn't as if lots of feet had worn the walkway
down, thus creating an obvious route. The environment
was quite barren; it was difficult to imagine that any
pleasure seekers, human or otherwise, would brave the
contours of this particular mountain for purposes of*

enjoyment, even though it did offer some spectacular views of the valleys below. And what other reason would anyone ever have for coming up here, he thought to himself, apart from needing somewhere to escape to - to be alone and isolated. Harvey continued to scavenge and gather along the way, plucking and picking at anything that looked edible. Yes, it was desolate and bleak but if you knew where to look, or if you were as interested and enthused as Harvey was, there were lots of diminutive surprises along the way. He was amassing quite a collection in his little satchel, so much so that it was beginning to burst at the seams. Each time he pulled a plant out of the ground, or yanked off a leaf or flower, he examined it in detail and smelt it intensely, handling it with the dexterity only a naturally talented cook could have. He turned to show Davey his latest addition; a pretty little stem of bell heather with pink and purple flowers and sharp leaves.

All of a sudden, an ear-splitting squeal came from up ahead. As they had paused briefly to admire the lovely bell heather, Stanley had continued on and was a few metres ahead. He was writhing around on the floor, oinking and screeching, grabbing at his hind leg. A large adder had been hiding next to the path, waiting, camouflaged among the rocks and weeds and mosses of the wilderness. It had leapt out at Stanley, digging its fangs in to his leg of pork. As soon as the bite was made, the adder skilfully wrapped itself around the struggling pig, with the intention of suffocating it. Stanley was quick to react however, and thrust his arm down by his side, preventing the snake from getting a firm hold around his belly. His leg throbbing with pain and his little lungs gasping for air, Stanley fought with the snake, prising its tight grip away from his chest, enabling himself to momentarily breathe in a swift intake of air. But the snake was powerful and slid silkily around Stanley's body, enveloping him almost completely. Even though his eyes were open, everything became dark as the thick muscles of the snake's underbelly enclosed around Stanley's head and face. Panic set in and Stanley found himself beginning to relax; not that he wanted to. He fought with all his might to push the snake away from his chest and throat so that he could take one more lifesaving breath. But it was no use. His arms went limp and the snake's grip tightened further still. Harvey and Davey rushed to his aid. It was nearly impossible to see Stanley. They didn't know where to start. So wrapped around Stanley was the snake that they could not for a moment find either end. They desperately dived on top of the writhing bundle and thrust their arms into the folds of the almighty reptile. Harvey managed to locate the snake's head and heaved with all his strength, slowly uncoiling the beast from around his brother. Davey grabbed its tail and together, they began to unravel the reptile, like pulling threads of shoes lace that had been knotted in many different ways. As the knots of the snake eventually began to loosen, the large and powerful snake was no match for the team of piglets it had attacked – once they had control over both ends, it had no leverage or momentum and was at their mercy. Stanley wrestled free of the monster's clasp as soon as he managed to work himself some space and, still *frantically puffing and panting, finally kicked himself free of the untangling serpent.*

Having secured the snake and covered its eyes by pressing a satchel onto its head in an attempt to somehow calm it, the pigs took a minute to recover from another ordeal. Stanley especially, whose leg was slightly reddened and swollen, needed time to assess his wound and get his breath back. The snake knew it was defeated and remained pinned down and calm. They decided that they would discard the snake and tend to the bite – Harvey said that some of the plants he'd collected had healing properties and that one in particular was known to soothe and numb infections. Still holding the snake's head, Harvey lifted it up and swung it round his head three times before releasing it behind them and to the right of the path as they looked back. It sailed through the air and landed in a heap next to a large bush, which it slithered under and curled into a swirl to nurse nothing more than a bit of pride.

"That bite is looking swollen, Stanley." said Davey.

"I know," he replied.

"I think we're gonna have suck the poison out before that plant of Harvey's is going to do any good." Davey suggested.

Three of them looked at each other with look of distaste and apprehension but without giving it a further thought, Davey and Harvey set about Stanley's leg, taking it in turns to suck the poison out of the wound. Squealing in pain, Stanley slapped at the heads of his brothers each time they got close to the bite, even though he knew they had to do it. After a few moments of slurping and spitting and head-slapping, the furore came to a halt and the three brothers stepped back from one another. Harvey then presented to Stanley the selection of trimmings from his satchel, which he had tied together expertly. Stanley took the parcel from his brother and rubbed it against his wound, wincing in pain. He squeezed the herbs and flowers together, drawing out the sap and fluids from within. Exactly as Harvey had said, the trimmings did indeed have a soothing affect upon the area of the bite.

"It is fortunate that all pigs have a very tough skin and a thick layer of fat just underneath it, which makes it very difficult for snakes to inject large amounts of poison into their bloodstream." Davey announced, slapping his thigh proudly and patting his brothers on the back.

Stanley was fine. He was battered and bruised, but tougher because of the experience and hopefully now more aware of predators lurking in the shadows. Harvey was very proud of himself and the healing parcel he had prepared for Stanley. He was also immensely pleased with how he had dispatched of the snake, thinking that not even Stanley could have sent the beast a further distance. Davey was concerned that at every turn, the group had come up against more and more frightening obstacles. He thought of what might be around the next corner. He wondered what unknown power was at work, trying to prevent them from reaching their goal. He prepared a large globule of sour tasting spit from his mouth and spat it out, the strong taste of the snake's poison still reminding him of the dangers that could lie ahead.

Back at Hillside Farm

It had been a quiet day on Hillside Farm. The revellers had taken the opportunity to recuperate, following the shenanigans from two nights before. Billy the Goat spent the day prancing about his field and chewing on its fresh grass, while Jonny the Cock strutted around his pen with a bit more vigour in his step. Regularly, they would chat with each other and recollect the highs and lows from Cynthia's party and discuss the possibility of another one being organised very soon. Cynthia had slept through the day once more but she awoke that evening feeling revived. Her hangover was softening and a good drink of water revitalised her. Claire brought her some freshly prepared veggies and other farmhouse leftovers, which Cynthia devoured hungrily. Afterwards, they sat at the dinner table downstairs and chatted over a pot of tea. Just the two of them. It was frustrating for Cynthia to realise that it had taken her to reach the lowest of lows – the act of her children walking out on her – in order for *her to realise the seriousness of her situation and to make some drastic and needed changes. How she hadn't realised sooner was beyond her and she couldn't understand how she had become so reliant on The Wolf and his deliveries.*

Claire was shocked to discover what The Wolf had been up to. The very fact that he had been visiting the farm undetected on so many occasions made her skin crawl. But the idea that he had been manipulating poor Cynthia all these years and Claire had done nothing to help made her feel terrible. Claire felt partly responsible for the collapse of Cynthia and Jeremy's relationship; if only she'd listened to the signs. Cynthia's demise was clear to see but all the parties and late night shenanigans made it look as though she was the problem, as though it was her attitude that needed to change. But all the while, she was in desperate need of a friend. Claire hah deserted her at the time she needed her most. Claire also felt responsible for the resulting journey undertaken by the pigs and the subsequent danger they were now in.

"How dare that Wolf sneak into the farm!" Claire shouted, slamming her hoof on the table and sending Cynthia's crockery sprawling across the room. "How dare he think that he can prey on vulnerable animals like that!"

"Calm down, Claire." Cynthia replied. "There's nothing we can do about it now."

"Calm down? Calm down? After all he's done? We can't just sit about and do nothing!" stated Claire, rising

above Cynthia and rearing angrily on her hind legs, knocking the lightshade from the ceiling. "We have to show solidarity and strength! We have to show that dastardly Wolf that you don't need his drugs – that you're better than that!"

"And how do you envisage doing that, Claire?" asked Cynthia, picking up the lightshade. Her demeanour became sombre and introverted. It was obvious that she was going to need all the help she could get if she was to gain control of her life back.

"We're going to get you back on your feet and right as rain in no time, you mark my words." encouraged Claire. She was already fussing in the kitchen, putting things away and making efforts to organise the chaotic living environment that Cynthia had been putting up with for so long. "I will speak to the other animals on the farm and we will all pull together, like the way it used to be, Cynthia. They all love you, you know that don't you?"

"Oh don't be so silly, how could they love a deadbeat like me?" she replied, wiping away a tear from her cheek. "I've caused nothing but damage and heartbreak for my family and I've put the whole farm at risk, encouraging that dirty Wolf to sneak in here so many times."

"That's all in the past now." Claire interrupted. "Solidarity and strength! That's what we need. Now up you get – I'll be damned if I'm going to do this all by myself." With that, Claire hoisted Cynthia up onto her feet and the two of them got started on turning Cynthia's life around, bit by bit.

A second night under the stars

Before the evening darkness had stolen the light of
day completely and while the sunset allowed them to see
just enough of their environs, Davey made the decision
to stop where they were and rest for the night. Just
below the first elevation of Seeker's Peaks, they settled
in and prepared to spend a second night under the stars.
The pigs discussed briefly the events of the day. Stanley
assessed his wound, licking it and pressing against the
swollen area, as if to push any remaining poison out of
his bloodstream. It was still very sore but he was
confident that it would be better by the morning. Harvey
was looking into the night sky, reminiscing of his earlier
heroics with the snake. Stanley was rubbing moist dirt
into his thick skin and he applied the mud to his brothers
where they lay before rustling around in the dirt,
preparing his 'bed' for the night. With only the leaves of
trees to act as shelter from the rain, the pigs experienced
a more uncomfortable and restless sleep than the

previous night. It took them a while to fall asleep as they tossed and turned, trying to find the most comfortable position. Eventually, they were asleep and intermittent snores and sleepy coughs echoed around the little camp they'd made for themselves.

And that's when he came. Silent as an insect, the large Wolf eased into the little clearing the pigs had found. His moist nose sniffed each of the pigs in turn. He took in the smell of youthful piglet, appreciating the young and tender morsels as they snoozed. He knew the pigs well and had stood over them as they slept many times before, during his visits to Hillside Farm. Very carefully, the Wolf approached Stanley and lowered his head so that his nostrils almost touched the snout of the pig. He could feel Stanley's quick breath on his sensitive nose. The Wolf's haggard face was enormous next to Stanley's little frame. Large stained teeth emerged as an evil smile began to spread across The Wolf's face. His powerful jaw opened and the Wolf leaned forward towards Stanley's neck. His whiskers brushed against the thick chops of the sleeping babe but he remained undisturbed, completely at the mercy of the monstrous beast. Wider still the jaws became and the Wolf's fangs took hold with expert precision. Ever so slowly, the Wolf pulled at the little satchel underneath Stanley's head. The little pig's ears flopped as the satchel was pulled away and his head tilted backward, resting gently on the soil. Taking two steps back, the Wolf returned to the centre of the clearing, Stanley's satchel dangling from mouth. He placed it on the floor and prowled over to Harvey, who had his back to the Wolf and snorted as he shuffled ever *so slightly. But forward still came the Wolf, removing Harvey's satchel with consummate ease. Davey's satchel was also positioned under his head, although he had looped the thin leather strap around his body so that he was actually lying on it. The Wolf sniggered, almost loudly enough to stir the little pigs. The Wolf recalled Cynthia talking of Davey's scholastic achievements during one of his very early visits to the farm, when she was still alert enough to know how her children were getting on at Farm School. He had spent a lot of time nurturing Cynthia as a potential client, earning her trust, learning exactly what to say to her to make her feel more relaxed. But Davey's cautious considerations were futile. As easily as he'd removed the previous two satchels, the Wolf unhooked the strap from around Davey's arm and slid it from underneath him, guiding the satchel out with it, as if removing the first piece in a Jenga puzzle.*

He could have eaten the three of them up there and then, but he wasn't hungry and they were nowhere near as fat and juicy as they would be in a few years. Wolf had watched them grow and was more than happy to let this three-course meal marinade for a few years longer. The Wolf rarely went without food; such were his predatory attributes. And such was his devious and evil nature, he was happy to allow the pigs to continue on their little trek, wherever it was going to take them. It delighted him that he was hindering their progress in some way. The Wolf picked up his newly acquired loot and left the clearing as silently as he'd entered it. He wasn't even interested in the contents of the satchels, simply discarding them in the nearby waters, watching them float away downstream, back in the direction from which the pigs had come. The Wolf was proud of his spiteful and meaningless act and he was looking forward to presenting a further obstacle to the little pigs at another point along their journey, should the opportunity arise.

He had been aware of their little escape from Hillside Farm right from the start; little did anyone other than Cynthia know, he was at the farm on that very night. Wolf was making a delivery and he left shortly before the three brothers had begun their own expedition. It was likely that it was the beast's scent that had got Ron so agitated out in the courtyard that morning. Having followed them from a distance for the duration of their adventure, all the while avoiding the watchful eye of Henry, the Wolf had decided that he would have a little fun with the naïve adventurers.

The following morning, the wind was still howling, as it had done throughout the night. At least this had brought with it a break in the rain. The skies were clear and sunlight shone down through the dancing leaves onto the faces of the brave little pigs, creating flickers of shadow and preventing them from concentrating on trying to sleep any longer. None of them had slept well, which made Stanley's discovery upon waking all the more surprising... and unsettling. The pain in his neck had been bothering him for a while now but he had been trying to ignore it, almost forcing himself to remain asleep. Opening his eyes, he took a moment to remember where he was and what he was doing. He blinked a number of times and felt the harsh surface of the woodland floor upon the side of his face. He was sure that he'd been using his satchel as a makeshift pillow. Satisfying himself with the idea that he must have rolled off it during the night, Stanley pushed himself up onto his elbow and looked around him. It wasn't there. Darting a worried look over to his brothers, he found their pillows were also missing. Their satchels were gone. They had nothing. No food, no water, no gadgets to help with the success of their mission. Their survival depended on these items.

"Wake up!" shouted Stanley. "Our bags! They're gone!" The other two pigs jumped up, awake at once, as they hadn't really been in a deep sleep anyway. Both reached for the space under their heads to grab their bags; both were shocked to learn that they weren't there. Confused and temporarily disorientated, they looked at Stanley.

"Someone's been here. Someone's taken our things!" said Stanley, standing above his brothers with a menacing look in his eyes. "Search the area."

The three pigs examined the immediate surroundings of where they were camped. They looked for broken branches; they smelt for unfamiliar scents; they surveyed in detail the grounds upon which they'd slept.

"Here!" Davey said urgently. He was crouched over a patch of moist ground near to the entrance of their encampment. Harvey and Stanley joined their brother and they all gathered round to look closely at what

Davey had found.

It was a footprint - faint and indistinct but clearly a footprint. It was a large central indentation with four smaller sections extending from it. At the end of each smaller section was a tiny, deep hole, obviously made by a claw of some kind. The footprint pointed away from where the pigs squatted and in the direction in which it faced, there could be seen a pathway, which weaved its way towards the highest tip of Seeker's Peaks. Whosever footprint it belonged to was large and was at this moment, somewhere up ahead of them. They would need to follow in the footsteps of this unknown beast. And probably confront it.

Just then, Henry, the carrier pigeon, flapped and flustered his way into the clearing, landing on a low branch close to the piglets.

"Now's not a good time for an update, Henry." said Stanley.

"It's not an update I'm here for." Henry replied. "I've been keeping Claire very much in the loop with regards to your adventures and she and I talked long into the night about the three of you. It's time you knew what you're getting yourselves into. If Claire's right about you, and she usually is, you're planning on finding your father."

More than just a journey

Henry told the three pigs about their father, Jeremy. He told them about how in love their parents used to be and how they grew apart. Henry told them of the evil Wolf and his role in their mother's depression, which ultimately, was the reason for them separating. He explained how the Wolf used to provide Cynthia with 'helpful and natural' sleeping pills and how dependent upon these she became.

The three little pigs sat and looked at each other. Each of them had the same teary and angry look in their eyes. A moment of silence settled among the group as they took in the new information they were being told. Henry was concerned that they were too young to handle such details but he remembered the promise he made to Claire. They had both agreed that the three pigs needed to know, particularly at this stage of their lives, when so much was at stake.

"I'm gonna find The Wolf and I'm gonna kill it!" shouted Stanley, rising from his seated position and standing above his brothers, looking down on them in a threatening manner. "I'm gonna make him pay! I'm going to make him wish he was never born!" his bellowing disturbed many of the mountain's hidden creatures and various rustles could be heard all around them as animals scampered away in fright and birds flew from their branches to find more serene trees in which to roost.

"We've got to be sensible about this Stan," pleaded Davey. "There's no point us trying to kill The Wolf by ourselves – that would be suicide."

"Yeah," agreed Harvey. "We've all heard the stories about Him. The missing lambs. The carcases and other remains he's left in his tracks over the years. He's a horrible monster and we don't have what it takes to match him, Stan."

So the drift of pigs and the carrier pigeon established that a further plan needed to be set out. Henry offered his services for the duration of their journey, stating that he would do everything within his powers to assist them. It was decided that Henry would carry out some scouting missions to check out what lay ahead of the vengeful pigs. With renewed vigour, the trio set out once again to track down their father. They had no supplies. They would have to fend for themselves even more so than when they first started off. Days of playing on the Farm seemed so far away. They would need to learn on the move and rely heavily on their instinct. And Henry; they'd *also have to rely on Henry.*

It was a day's hike to the top of Seeker's Peaks. The rain from the night before had ceased but the hillside was still soaked and the trail was wet and slippery. Davey spread a little mud across his cheeks - a double line just under the eyes. Harvey and Stanley looked at him inquisitively, then looked at each other, shrugged their shoulders and applied the war paint to their own faces. An old piece of material, caught on the low-hanging branch of a nearby tree, flapped invitingly in the wind. Davey yanked it down forcefully and tore it into three equal parts. In unison, the rags were ceremoniously folded and placed across the foreheads of each pig, before being tied tightly at the back of the head. Without their satchels, they would need to be creative and resourceful. Stanley grabbed a long branch from another tree, snapped it off and removed all the excess from it, leaving a sturdy off-cut that would make a good staff. Harvey foraged the immediate area for anything nutritious and found some nettles and mushrooms that he knew were beneficial; it wasn't that pigs needed to worry about being poisoned. He'd learnt that his brothers had become quite fussy after getting used to his culinary skills. Fortunately, he still had his red neckerchief around his neck so he untied that and used it has a pouch. Davey opted for a thick, short piece of branch that he thought would do well as a dagger type instrument. He used a conveniently shaped rock to sharpen one end of the tool and was pleased to see a droplet of blood appear at the end of his trotter when he test-pricked himself with it when it was finished. A smile of satisfaction spread across his face. Henry watched in bewilderment before flying off to explore the trail ahead. He was quietly confident that these piglets were going to destroy anything that lay in their path.

Manoeuvring through the hilltop with semi-expert precision, the group made it to the top of Seeker's Peak with no problem. It was a tough slog but they stood triumphantly at the summit and scanned the view. They could make out Hillside Farm in the far away distance - the farmhouse, the garage in which the tractor was kept. Even their pigsty and Claire's barn and field could be spotted. It was a humbling moment. They embraced each other and, for a second, the three pigs felt like they were back home, playing and sauntering around the farm's outskirts under the watchful eye of their surrogate mother, Claire. However, Claire wasn't with them. Apart from Henry, they were all alone and as they breathed in the fresh mountain air, the scale of their mission became apparent. So far they had come. And yet so much further they had to go, so much more they had to do. Jeremy, their long lost father, was rumoured to have spent much of his early days as an escapee in the caves and fissures of Springfield Mount. The daunting highland area was vast and eerie. A long winding route led towards the next apex, with a large break halfway along. It was clear that although the pigs wouldn't have to climb any higher, their passage to Springfield Mount was going to be their most testing challenge so far. Up here, they were at the mercy of the elements; it was a raw and wild environment.

Springfield Mount

Standing just a little higher than Seeker's Peaks but far more barren and inhospitable, Springfield Mount was renowned for being unrelenting to even the most experienced of hikers, let alone three little pigs. Still embracing, the brothers spoke about their fondest recollections of the Farm. Distant memories of freedom and joy before Cynthia became unhinged. Times of excitement in discovering secret parts of the grange that they were not supposed to go to. Games of hide and seek; drinking thirstily from the mud pools, even though Claire told them it would make them sick. Despite all these wonderful remembrances, none of them could remember their father. Releasing from their huddle, the adventurers stood in a line, shoulder to shoulder, gazing across the ragged rocks and along the searching trail. They could see Henry swooping and somersaulting through the air, sporadically darting high into the sky and occasionally hovering in the airstream.

Stanley thrust his newly formed staff into the ground. It was a symbol of defiance against what lay ahead of them and a signal to his comrades that from now on, they would need to be extra vigilant. The pigs began to march. Flurries of wind blew against them and their eyes squinted against the returning rain that now fell cold on their faces. Swollen clouds had assembled above them, seemingly out of nowhere and without warning. A cloudy and threatening darkness fell about them as they traipsed through the sodden turf and navigated the hazardous rocks. The path became narrow as it began to run alongside the cliff edge and the brothers adopted a single file formation, keeping over to the left, away from the brink of what had become an unnerving overhang. Stanley led from the front; constantly muttering away to himself about his hatred for The Wolf and steadying himself with his staff. He did his best to ignore the trickles of blood that were now beginning to squeeze out through his knuckles as the stick he tightly held cut into his palms. Harvey remained close behind his leader and edged along watchfully, keeping to the cold, rocky wall that had now risen up on their left. Davey took up the rear, keeping an anxious scrutiny over the narrow walkway and sheer drops to his right. He thought to himself that Harvey certainly wouldn't be handing out any mushrooms or nettles any time soon. One slip would lead to certain death.

Sure enough, it happened. Due to the huddled nature of their formation, it became frequently more difficult to pinpoint secure tractions on the path. The wind was battering against them form all directions and risking a

*loose foothold seemed to be the lesser of two evils.
Harvey stepped on a larger slab of rock that appeared
solid, but it immediately gave way, sliding off the edge of
the path and tumbling down the near vertical face.
Down Harvey went with the rock, letting out a squeal of
terror as, for a moment, he felt weightlessness. As quick
as a flash, Stanley pivoted and lunged towards his falling
comrade. He flung his staff out over the edge of the cliff
and a pair of trotters clasped tightly onto it as Stanley
landed heavily on his belly, supporting the full weight of
Harvey as his brother was suspended from the end of the
wooden pole. The stricken pig dangled in open air, an
emptiness of hundreds of feet below him. Their eyes met,
wide, terrified and determined. Stanley began to shake
with the build-up of lactic acid screaming through his
arms. Despite the fact that he was an extremely fit and
active piglet, he was still just a piglet and his recent
adventures and lack of food had made him weaker.
Trotters, that were just seconds earlier, clasped tightly
around each end of the staff, began to slowly slip and
unravel. The rugged pole cut deeper still into his palms
and Stanley began to moan and growl deeply, grinding
his teeth together and wincing against the pain and the
struggle. Davey hadn't reacted as quickly as Stanley but
he immediately saw the urgency of the situation and he
too dived onto his belly, grabbing hold of the staff, which
was now bending under the weight. Together, the
wriggling and screeching pig was hauled back up to
safety. They lay in a crumpled heap, panting heavily.
Henry landed just a few metres ahead of them at the
opening of a semi-circular clearing and stared at the*

group, expressionless.

"Thanks for the help!" jested Stanley, breathlessly.

"Call yourself a carrier pigeon?" panted Davey. "You could've flown down here and 'carried' Harvey to safety for us!" He even had the energy to mimic two sets of speech marks with his trotters, to emphasise his pun.

Slowly, a patter of laughter began to emerge from the throats of the three survivors. Gradually, the laughter grew and as they glanced across at each other, they somehow found the energy to laugh a little harder, until eventually, the pigs were writhing in hysterical hilarity, rolling far too close to the edge of the crag for Henry's comfort and slapping each other's shoulders with delight. Although it seemed to Henry that this was not the best time or place to share a joke, it dawned on him that the pigs probably hadn't laughed much recently and it was good to get it out of their system. He too began to coo and chortle away at the absurdity of the situation before him and he thought to himself that he must remember that one the next time he was out with his friends. In a way, it was likely that they were all laughing, not just at the ordeal they had already been through, but also at the ordeal they still had to get through.

The tough little pigs were scratched and bruised. But their spirit was never stronger. There's nothing like surviving a near death experience to get your feet back on the ground and your priorities straightened out. Helping one another to their feet, they made their way to the glade in which Henry was still waiting. Before them was one of the most magnificent scenes they had ever set eyes upon. They stood afoot a towering waterfall and it was only as they stepped onto the rock-strewn clearing that the sound of the crashing water hit them. It was deafening. Henry pointed a wing over to the right, indicating the only way around the latest obstacle that stood in their way; a steep set of steps that seemed to lead down into the waterfall itself.

"Don't worry!" Henry shouted over the noise. "It's quite safe! You just have to go down the steps, then behind the waterfall and back up over there!"

"What do you mean 'you'?" barked Harvey. "Don't you mean 'we'?"

Henry waddled over to Harvey. "I'm a pigeon Harvey. I have wings." And with that, the bird flew out over the waterfall and landed in a lonely tree on the other side. "Come on!" he shouted across, beckoning them with a flap of his wings.

Down the steep stairs they went. Down, lower alongside the rushing water. They grabbed onto weeds and pushed against jagged rocks to steady themselves. Further down, the steps turned into the mountain and back on themselves. As the pigs ventured further, they saw the path that led behind the white wall of water. From here, the noise seemed far more muffled and they almost felt secure, as if the waterfall was protecting them. They strode along the walkway, holding their cupped hands out into the foamy wall and gulping down huge swallows of ice-cold spring water. Finding themselves at the base of the route leading up the other side of the waterfall, the pigs looked up and saw the tree that Henry had landed in. It was empty. Henry was nowhere to be seen.

"Where's he gone?" asked Stanley, craning his neck, looking skywards.

His brothers shrugged and continued upwards. Hoisting themselves up with the same types of weeds and rocks that had supported them on the way down minutes earlier, they reached the lonesome tree on which Henry had landed. He had indeed vanished. They searched the cloudy skies for anything; some clue of where he was. Nothing. The thick grey clouds moved slowly across the sky and they heard a faint roll of thunder in the distance and moments later, a slight flash of lightning from somewhere lit up the horizon. The rain began to fall heavier. Before them was the top of Springfield Mount. It was relatively flat and there wasn't much happening. Despite the windy conditions, it looked moderately calm because there weren't many trees or bushes that would usually be thrashing around in this sort of weather. The best indication of the force of the wind was the rain seemed to be falling almost horizontally. The few trees that stood about the area were short in height and short of leaves too. Shrubs and bushes sat around in groups and these were the only things that gave any colour to the scene, which stood before the three pigs. They had much preferred the serenity of the base of Wakeman's Hill, with its delicate hillside flowers and different types of trees. Davey remembered looking up at Wakeman's Hill and hearing the sounds of running water and birds singing. In stark contrast, Springfield Mount had no such resonances. The wind and rain combined to create the only noise they could hear – the rain lashed down loudly and the wind whirled around the little pigs' ears.

"What do we do now?" asked Harvey, calling out above the noise of the wild weather.

"This is where he's meant to be!" shouted Davey. "This is where Henry told us that Dad ended up."

"Here?" said Stanley, a confused look on his face. "There's nothing here."

"Oh you'd be surprised!" said a deep, rough voice from behind them.

The three pigs jumped and turned around, startled. In front of them stood a huge, boar. They looked at him, bewildered and astonished. Each of them knew immediately that it was their father. Jeremy stared back at his children, looking deep into their eyes as he did so. Before him were three little piglets. They had a determined look in their eyes and each of them wore a dark green Rambo-style headband. They looked battered and bruised and ready for action. Smudges of mud on their faces seemed to indicate that the trio had prepared for their journey by smearing war paint across their cheeks. One held a long stick proudly in one hand, another clenched a sharp wooden dagger and the third dangled a red pouch from his grasp. They were a sight to behold that was for sure. A faint smile formed at one corner of his mouth.

Jeremy

"I think you three had better come with me." Jeremy said, calmly. They were still speechless. They followed him silently as he trudged through the saturated ground, creating his own path across the desolate countryside. Gentle peaks and troughs of the landscape revealed elements of Springfield Mount that were originally hidden from the three pigs when they had stood beneath Henry's tree, moments earlier. They came across jagged, rocky clearings and cave openings that led into complete darkness. They also walked through coarse bushes and brambles, occasionally stopping as Jeremy sniffed the air and took a moment to listen to any sounds he might hear. As they ascended one of the many little peaks in question, the enormous pig froze. Like a game of follow my leader, the three little pigs were immediately statue like; they had become extremely good at this during the course of their travels. Jeremy's head sniffed the air again, much in the same way as Ron had done back at the farm, what seemed like so long ago now.

"Your friend has returned." said Jeremy, softly.

They all looked up and saw the pigeon descending upon them. From his mouth dangled some peculiar shapes that none of them could make out. As he got closer, the three brothers gawped at the bird, not quite believing what they were looking at. He swooped down, expertly landing on the thickest branch of a low and bare bush nearby.

"Our satchels!" exclaimed Davey, delighted in the hope that he would be reunited with his treasured little items.

Giving Jeremy a cautious look, Henry dropped the satchels on the ground and began to explain that he had planned to fly back to Hillside Farm to keep Claire, and therefore Cynthia, in the loop about how they were getting on. Jeremy's interest heightened at the mention of his long lost beloved and he shuffled a little closer, his gigantic frame giving Henry some welcome cover from the gusty winds. Harvey passed around the last of his mushrooms and nettles from his neckerchief while Henry continued and it turned out that as he was soaring above where the pigs had spent their first night, he spotted something strange in the stream and dived down to have a quick look. The satchels were entangled together, floating and caught up in some weeds that were growing out of the water. Knowing their importance to the little pigs, and particularly how proud Davey was of his little mirror, Henry thought it best to retrieve the leather pouches and bring them back *immediately to their rightful owners. Of course, this meant that Claire was now completely unaware of how her babies were getting on and without an update soon, she and Cynthia would soon begin to worry.*

Davey picked up the satchels, put his over his shoulder and fastened it to his belly, before handing the other two to his brothers. He told Henry that he'd done the right thing and that he should return to Cynthia and Claire to prevent them from worrying unnecessarily. Jeremy watched his son inquisitively, surprised at the confidence which seemed to ooze from the little pig. He seemed to be making decisions without hesitation, taking it upon himself to assume responsibility for the group. And the trust that his brothers had in him was clear to see; both of them listened intently to his instructions and responded immediately and without question.

"Tell them where we are and that we've found Dad." *he said, sternly. "Tell them that we'll be home soon but that we've got some unfinished business to take care of first."*

Henry was about to fly off but Jeremy stopped him with a raise of a large, powerful trotter.

"Tell Cynthia I still love her." he said, very seriously.

An almost awkward silence fell on the group for a brief moment and the three little pigs looked at each other and started to smile, childishly.

"Get on with it!" shouted Jeremy, embarrassed. He swished at the bird and Henry flapped into the air and was gone. Upon turning around, he gazed down at his

children. *"We've got so much to talk about; I know I have so many unanswered questions, I'm sure you do as well. That time will come. I'm so proud of all of you – how you managed to find me so far away from home. I meant what I said just then. I do still love your mother very much. Leaving was the hardest thing I've ever done and each day since hasn't gotten any easier. At the time, I made a decision that I thought was best for you and Cynthia. You must all understand that. I never wanted to leave and I'd give anything to have you all back. It's just as each day passed, the idea of coming home became more and more difficult to imagine. Days turned into weeks, weeks turned into months and before I knew, I was different. My children."* Jeremy whispered, placing a huge paw upon each of their little heads. Harvey could have sworn that he saw tears in his father's eyes but before he could tell for sure, the huge beast turned and began to trundle along the rocky pathway.

Without another word, the foursome continued onwards and the three pigs had a chance to reflect on what their father had said. Each of them was grateful that they had found their father and that he was safe and seemingly well. They were also relieved that he had accepted them. Only days earlier, it had crossed their minds that Jeremy may not even recognise or acknowledge them. The silent meander also gave them time to consider what next. What did they want from their father now that they had found him? It was clear that he was glad to see them but was his life so different now that it would be too difficult a task to face for him to return home with them? They had come all this way;

been through so much. Davey smiled as he recalled the huddle upon the crest of Seeker's Peaks; how the three of them had reminisced of home. Stanley mused over the reasons why they had started out on this journey; to find their father and bring him home. They were closer to that ideal than ever and a tingling of excitement came over him as he pictured his mother's face at the entrance to their pigsty when they finally returned home. Harvey clasped at a pretty shrub, the likes of which he had never seen before. He examined it carefully, gently cradling it in his trotters before easing it slowly out of the ground, roots still intact. He found comfort in rubbing the smooth texture of the thick little leaves and it brought him back to days on Hillside Farm when he loitered under the farmhouse kitchen window, watching the chef at work. The three pigs followed their father in silence, a sense of togetherness encapsulating the trio more than ever before.

Jeremy finally stopped at what looked like an ordinary bush, just like many of the others they had passed along the way. This particular bush was larger than any of the others and it grew out of the side of a raised mound of earth. Jeremy brushed through an especially dense section of the bush and disappeared. Stanley didn't hesitate and followed his father into the darkness beyond the bramble. Harvey and Davey were a little unsure but they weren't exactly going to wait outside to be persuaded to go in. Through the bushes they went and found Stanley waiting for them at the entrance of a long tunnel. A few steps ahead, Jeremy was already tramping into the darkness. The befuddled pigs followed, rounding a bend before the tunnel opened up into a large well-lit room. Candles that hung from the walls burned brightly and their constant flickering creating an eerie yet homely atmosphere. It was a very simple design; the ceiling just high enough for Jeremy to stand. A darker section of the cave where the flickers of the candles did not reach was a great pile of leaves and ferns; undoubtedly comfortable sleeping quarters. Opposite the 'bedroom', positioned in between two of the three wall-lights, the wall had been dug out to create a good-sized arch in which a healthy fire burned brightly. A large box of firewood sat to the left of the fire and Jeremy stoked the embers before throwing two more logs into the flames. He motioned for his children to sit down at a sturdy, wooden table that looked like it had been skilfully crafted out of different kinds of wood. It was the centrepiece of the cave and a fine item of furniture, fit for a king. It needed to be large enough to accommodate its maker but Davey thought to himself who else might have sat here. It wasn't as if his father was turning visitors away and there weren't exactly a huge number of potential guests in the vicinity. Perhaps Jeremy liked the idea that someday, the four chairs that accompanied the table would have a purpose. They were of the same handmade style and, upon sitting, Stanley thought to himself how comfortable they were. Goblets of water that Jeremy scooped out of a spring from the wall of the room were placed in front of the thirsty pigs and they drank eagerly from them. Harvey gazed around in wonder at how neat and tidy everything was. Having spent all his living memory in a literal pigsty, he found it strange sitting in the relative luxury of a well-kept dwelling such as their father's cave.

The spring particularly took his attention; how the shape of the bowl had been forged out of the mud or rock and how it seemed to be a continuous flow of water. He'd only just noticed that the cave was silent apart from the occasional crackle of splintering wood in the fire, and the trickle of water as it ran down a carefully chiselled groove along the wall of the cave, before gathering in the makeshift basin. The clever design allowed for the water to flow out of the basin once it was full, ensuring that Jeremy had a constant supply of drinking water. The three brothers spent a few moments taking in the scene and each of them seemed quite shell-shocked to have discovered how their father had been living. Jeremy was hunched over a smaller table under the third candle and upon the surface sat numerous bowls and containers. Harvey noticed how well organised the food supplies were but before he had a chance to investigate further, Jeremy turned and approached the table holding a tray. After placing a few bowls of various snacks down on the table, Jeremy joined his sons and they spent a moment sitting together in further silence.

Long into the night, the newly reunited family members talked. They talked about each other's lives, their interests and hobbies, likes and dislikes. They got to know each other – they'd never really had a chance to do that before and, on occasion, it got rather emotional. Jeremy would excuse himself from the table, teary eyed *and making excuses that it might be down to the onions he had chopped earlier. Davey, Harvey and Stanley all had their moment of sensitivity too and by the end of it, they were all a bit wiser and certainly more capable of accessing and expressing their emotions than before. Each of them learned something new about the other and although he hadn't really been in their lives for very long, the three pigs came to the conclusion that Jeremy had a caring personality and it was this that was the reason for him leaving. He cared about Cynthia and his family so much that he was prepared to leave in order for them to survive. Jeremy had watched his relationship with his childhood sweetheart decline rapidly and after doing everything in his power to save it, he realised that he had to give her space. Though he tried to tell her on numerous occasions how much he loved her, they were never able to talk without things turning into a full blown argument. Every time he tried to patch things up, it seemed as though Cynthia was too tired or too busy. It was all too clear now just how manipulative the Wolf had been and Jeremy sat at the table in deep thought. He was thinking about how different things might have been, about how wonderful his life could have been and how amazing his relationship with his children might have been, if it hadn't been for that blasted Wolf. Even so, Jeremy felt the sense of guilt upon his enormous shoulders, weighing him down with every breath. The conversation with the piglets had made him feel better though, lighter even. He hadn't had anyone to talk to for a long time and he had found it hard at first, but as the early morning drew nearer, Jeremy found it easier to* speak his thoughts; to understand how he truly felt. And in turn, this made it easier to work out what he was going to do next. But for now, this moment, this night, would be dedicated to his children. He yearned to find out more about them. So little time they had spent in each other's company and so much they had discovered already.

The little pigs told their father of the events of their adventures. They explained about the family of foxes that they had to scare away. Stanley was quick to highlight the ferocity with which he'd brought the heavy stone down onto the head of the large fox. Davey enthused about his clever little trick with the mirror, which blinded the fox, giving Stanley the time he needed. Harvey described in detail how his accurate throwing of the carefully selected nuts, enabled the whole plan to go so smoothly. They told Jeremy about the snake and how strong Stanley had been in wrestling with it, how brave Davey was when he peeled the snake from around Stanley's body and how quick-thinking Harvey had been in throwing the snake away. Finally, they spoke of Harvey's fall on the cliff top leading to Springfield Mount, when they worked together so effectively as a team to save his life. In return, the proud little piglets heard of their father's own journey, staring with how he escaped from the veterinarian's clinic. They learned that he spent his first few nights on or near the top of Wakeman's Hill. He told them of his efforts to build a shelter of some kind. Despite his broken heart, he was still determined to survive, so he gathered twigs and weeds and straw to make somewhere for him to sleep. It took him all day to gather enough materials and all night to build it. Unfortunately, it didn't stay up for that long – as soon as he lay his head down to sleep, a slight gust of wind came along and blew the whole shelter away. Jeremy explicated that over the next few days, he made his way to the heights of Seeker's Peaks. He explained that, once there, he tried again to build somewhere for him to stay. This time, he chose more sturdy materials; wood, branches and vines. This new and improved shelter was more effective than the first one he'd built. However, the inevitable happened when, on a stormy night, the shelter was battered by the elements and, after a great deal of huffing and puffing, it was left in tatters. And that, Jeremy concluded, was how he ended up in the cave in which they all sat. It was the perfect shelter; sturdy, well hidden and, once a fire had been lit, warm and cosy. As barren as Springfield Mount was, it had provided Jeremy with everything he needed to survive; he just had to learn to be resourceful.

Claire and Cynthia ring the changes

By this point, Henry had been at Cynthia's sty for a while and was still overwhelmed by how clean it was. She and Claire, along with some of the other farm animals had worked wonders with the place. It had been emptied, cleaned and everything had been returned with a better consideration to where it should be – there was a real Feng Shui about how her new home had been designed. Cynthia was energised and optimistic – two things she hadn't been in a long time. Henry sat them both down and relayed to them the information of how the three travellers were getting on. The news that her children were safe and that Jeremy was still in love with her had resulted in an extra spring in her step and she was busying herself about the house, puffing pillows in the lounge area and rearranging her best china. She wasn't going to use the cheap stuff anymore; things were going to be different around here from now on.

The experience of returning to Cynthia's newly

decorated home also had an uplifting effect on Henry. He was so happy to see the two of them getting on so well after so long. He whistled and cooed in appreciation as he darted from room to room to see what changes they had made. When he had finished exploring, he perched outside Cynthia's front door and scanned the farm. He thought how funny it was that things just seemed to be carrying on as normal, while the heroic little piglets were out venturing on the quest of their young lives. The door to the sty was open as Cynthia was airing the place and Claire popped out to join Henry. She issued the bird with some simple instructions and presented him with a few tasty rations to carry with him back to the journeying pigs. Cynthia joined them and handed Henry a piece of paper – a message for Jeremy – a little note that Henry was under strict instructions to put directly into the hand of her suitor; it obviously contained some details that were not appropriate for the youthful piglets.

"Bring my babies home." said Cynthia, tearfully.

Henry flapped into the air, turning before he left to give them both a reassuring look. He spun round and set off while the two newfound friends stood side by side and watched him disappear into the sky. When he was completely out of sight, Claire straightened up and took in a huge draw of breath. She looked at Cynthia and smiled. They both sensed that this might just be the beginning of a fresh start, for Cynthia, the piglets and for Jeremy. And also for the farm itself. Claire recalled how things used to be when the piglets were very young. She remembered how all the farm animals had gathered round at their birth to be with the family. Back then all the animals supported each other and looked out for each other. There was an element of sadness in Cynthia's face. Perhaps she would never lose that hidden expression; perhaps it would always be there. The Wolf had done so much damage; maybe some of it was irreparable. One thing that Claire did know was that Cynthia was going to need her and the other animals more than ever. Cynthia's lifestyle would have to change and in order for that to happen, the entire farm would need to be in support. After setting Cynthia the unenviable task of completing the remaining house chores (she knew it would be best of Cynthia was kept busy – she had to have something to keep her mind occupied at this stage of her rehabilitation, if you could call it that), Claire left to go and speak with Ron, Billy and Johnny. Ron would need to be extra vigilant from now on and make sure that Hillside Farm was safe. He would need to be on twenty-four look out; alert even when he slept. Billy and Johnny, on the other hand, would need to be prepared for the fact that there would be no more parties. Claire thought it a good idea to instruct them both to set their minds to coming up with some alternative pass times that everyone on the farm could be involved with. She also thought it would be nice if they made some preparations for return of the three pigs. She wasn't sure how any of them would react to the news that Jeremy was on his way home.

Henry finds the cave

Despite the extra weight, he flew faster than his wings could carry him, using all the skills that a highly experienced carrier pigeon possesses. He arrived at the point at which he'd left Jeremy flapping at him with embarrassment over his instruction to tell Cynthia that he still loved her. Landing in the very same bush, he looked around and recalled in which direction the group had walked. Confident in his assessment of the situation, he flew high into the sky and surveyed the area. The sun was up, beaming across the hilltops and not too far away, Henry could make out what he thought was faint clouds of black smoke. There were no other indications of activity so he flew over in search of his companions. Even though he was a pigeon, he had an eagle eye for detail and he could pinpoint tracks and footprints from a good height. Identifying the deep footmarks that obviously belonged to a very heavy creature, Henry soon located the entrance to the cave and managed to rustle his way through the bushes and down the tunnel to where the pigs were camped. The four of them were getting ready, preparing themselves for the day ahead and they all jumped as Henry flew in unannounced. Despite the fact that they had already eaten breakfast, they were more than happy to tuck into the grubs and delights that Henry had carried with him.

"I haven't tasted mum's cooking in ages!" exclaimed Harvey, enthusiastically wolfing down a roasted carrot.

"Err, I think Claire made these." stated Henry, cautiously. "Cynthia has been too busy redecorating her home to have cooked anything."

Jeremy coughed and spluttered at the mention of Cynthia getting to grips with revamping the sty and the three brothers looked up at the pigeon, the same surprised look on their faces. Cynthia hadn't been one for DIY, even when she was younger, let alone at this difficult time of her life.

"I think she's looking forward to having you all back at home, together." continued Henry. "Which is where I assume we are now going?" he asked.

"No chance!" said Stanley, a vengeful look on his face. " We've got a job to do before we can go home; a score to settle. We've been up all night talking and we've decided that until that Wolf is gone no-one is safe."

"We know where his den is." Davey joined in. "Dad has had sightings of him over the years and he's followed him a few times."

"But it's not going to be easy." said Jeremy, rising from his seated position at the head of the table. When he walked on his hind legs, Jeremy stood over seven feet and was a fearsome sight. "This wolf has lived in the wild all his life. He's a survivor. He knows the environment and he's not stupid. He's also extremely dangerous, particularly when he's threatened. I've seen with my own eyes how powerful and ferocious he can be. I've watched him stalk his prey. He hunts alone and he's very effective. His den is located near Wakeman's Hill – he probably stole your satchels and he must have dumped them in the nearby stream."

"But why would he take our satchels and then just throw them in the river?" asked Stanley.

"Because he's evil." answered Davey. " I bet he got some sick and twisted kick out of it. He knew who we were. Maybe he worked out what we were doing out there. My guess is that he just wanted to make things more difficult for us than they already were."

A calming silence fell on the group as they collected themselves and focused on the next part of what was no longer an adventure but a mission; a matter of life or death.

The way back

Jeremy was a large, fearful beast and had survived alone in his environment for a long time now. His sons were naïve and inexperienced in comparison, but over the course of their journey, they had learnt about teamwork and loyalty, about honour and trust. The four of them would now need to work together as a true family if they were to defeat the horrible Wolf. As they headed out towards the waterfall, Jeremy would occasionally stand on his hind legs to get a better view up ahead. Towering over seven feet gave him an almost unobstructed three hundred and sixty degree assessment of his surroundings. The piglets were watching him all the time, copying his movements and soaking up of the lessons of survival all the while. As Jeremy stood next to the lone and bare tree at the height of the waterfall, Henry swooped down and landed on his shoulder. Davy, Harvey and Stanley were peering over the edge, marvelling at the sheer power of the cascades of water. While the piglets were admiring the waterfall, Henry handed Cynthia's note to Jeremy. Keeping to his word, the piglets were unaware of the delivery of this particular message and Jeremy understood that this was a private matter. He took the note and placed it into one of the small pouches attached to his belt; he would read it later while his children were preoccupied or asleep.

Down the steps of the waterfall they went, through the back of the wall of water and up the flight of stairs to the other side. A gritty determination had descended upon the group. They spoke little and when they did, they used hushed whispers and simple statements. Each of their minds was focused on one thing and one thing only - to seek out and destroy the Wolf. The group approached the narrow pathway where just the day before, Harvey had needed the assistance of his brothers to help him climb back up after nearly slipping to his certain death. This time, they strode along the footway with seemingly no concern for the vertical drop on their left. The weather had been relatively calm since they had left the cave and it was only now that they were perched high up on the ledges of Springfield Mount that the gusts of wind became stronger and the rain noticeably colder. But still they walked, unmoved by the force of the gales and unaffected by the icy precipitation that battered their chops. Retracing the steps of their journey, the piglets continued to move as a group, edging ahead or to the left and right, checking for movements or signs of life. They also kept a watchful eye out for any footprints or disturbances that may have given them any clue as to the Wolf's whereabouts. It was unlikely that a predator such as he would leave any trace behind but they weren't going to leave anything to chance. Soaked and being ferociously blown about in the high winds, Henry somehow managed to maintain a reasonably steady position, from which he could make out the path that lay ahead of his comrades. He soared and hovered, flipped and swooped, skilfully fighting against the powerful gusts and resisting the urge to find cover in the solitude of a dense tree.

The rain continued to pour. The winds were relentless. Underfoot became more treacherous than ever. The dark skies appeared swollen and angry. Thunder clapped loudly and lightning seemed to strike simultaneously. The entire group of warriors found themselves moving more closely together and even Jeremy jumped with fright at the more violent thunderclaps and winced at the strobe-like flashes of the lightning. The storm raged. The pigs battled onwards, traversing the perilous Seeker's Peaks with fortitude and purpose. Occasionally, one of them would fall due to exhaustion or slip on the rain-sodden surface. But every time, there was a brother to pick them up. Every time there was a supportive trotter on the shoulder or an encouraging nudge from behind. Although they hadn't spoken in ages, they were communicating more effectively than ever before. As the darkness of late evening set around them, they descended the lower of the two hilltops of Seeker's Peaks and they could just make out the silhouette of Wakeman's Hill below them a fair distance away.

They had trekked all day in the most gruelling and arduous conditions imaginable. It was time to rest. Not that they would be able to sleep. Too pumped up on adrenaline to sleep, and too focused on what they had set out to do, the four pigs slumped in a tight circle and huddled as best they could. Arms linked and legs interlocked, they protected themselves from the wind that had been battering them with increasing strength all afternoon. There were no signs of it letting up. As if being poured from a large jug above them, rain fell onto the heads of the tired quartet and ran down their necks and backs, onto the floor on which they sat. A large puddle began to form but the pigs didn't move. Despite their now soldier-like status and even appearance, they hadn't forgotten that they were pigs and that their favourite place to be was in a big pool of thick mud. As the thunder crashed around them, the flashes of lightning lit up the circle of faces and as they looked at each other, each of them began to smile. Smiles of pain and sickened enjoyment. Smiles of the memories of good times and struggles. Smiles of lost years that they might have enjoyed together as a family. The smiles turned to sneers. Sneers of hate and revenge. Sneers turned to scowls. Scowls of heartache and treachery. Without sleeping, the pigs rested. They seemed to enter a mental state, as if they were hypnotised, zoning in and out of semi consciousness, yet wide-awake and alert to their surroundings at all times.

The night passed slowly. Not an inch did the team budge within their pool of mud. As the sun began to rise, waking the flowers and birds from their drenched slumbers, the pigs began to stir. One by one, they unlocked their legs and arms from each other and spent some time wallowing in the mud, stretching and flexing.

They were a sight to see. The three small piglets, each with a small satchel strapped to their bellies and a Rambo-style strap of material tied around their heads, dipped and dunked in the muddied waters. The large dominant male pig was enormous. He arched his back, stretching his powerful arms high into the lower branches of the trees above him, his own belt with various little pouches attached, strapped round his waist. Once more, with very little discussion among the group, they prepared to move on and, after a final check about themselves and some last minute touch-ups of war paint, they were ready to roll.

"Fly home, Henry." Jeremy said. "There's nothing more you can do here. Tell Cynthia we'll be home soon." Henry tried to object but Jeremy held up his trotter and looked at Henry, right in his eyes. "You must go. They need you now." Henry's shoulders sunk and his head lowered, but he knew Jeremy was right.

"Get him." he said. And he was gone.

Wolf

Always busy and always thinking, always scheming, the Wolf was returning from a recent venture to the northwest of Wakeman's Hill. Cynthia was by no means his only 'client'. The Wolf had spent a long time researching all the farms within the area, getting himself acquainted with the comings and goings of how all the little businesses worked. On this particular morning, he was on his way back from Buck Lane Grange, a quaint and cute little farmstead that was similar to Hillside Farm in many ways. For the Wolf, it was the same old story. All he had to do was wait for a hint of weakness to show in the character of any one of the many farm animals at his disposal. He would move from farm to farm, sneaking and spying, getting to know the families. Everyone becomes vulnerable at some stage in their lives, no matter who or what they are. Sheep, cows, hens, goats and of course pigs, to name a few, can all experience forms of distress or depression of kind. And the Wolf had an excellent sense of when the time was right to move in on his prey and offer them a way out. In return, the Wolf would have free reign of the countryside. He was allowed to roam the neighbourhood without being questioned by any of the animals that spotted him, which was rare, because the Wolf had something to use against almost all of the other animals. If it wasn't someone's sister or brother, uncle or auntie, it was someone's mum or even daughter that the Wolf was 'providing' for, and if he was wronged in anyway, he would be able to ruin even further the lives of those concerned. Or even worse, he would be able to end the lives of those concerned. So the Wolf was basically untouchable and had been for a long time. He had everyone in his furry pocket and he wasn't about to give up on his do-what-I-like lifestyle without putting up a fight.

And it had been the same story for generations. Wolf after Wolf. The long line of the Wolf family had terrorised the entire countryside as far back as the oldest bull could remember. The Wolf grew up in a dark den, hidden within the charming surroundings of Wakeman's Hill. He was lovingly raised by the notorious Mr and Mrs Wolf; a vile and despicable couple who were known throughout the area for their relentless pursuit of evil. They seemed only happy when they were surrounded by pain and disgruntlement of their own doing. Yes, they loved their only child very much. This only resulted in a greater determination on their part to raise the most awful and dreadful character that they could muster. With their 'love', it was guaranteed that the Wolf would grow up to be the most appalling and fearsome member *of the entire generation of the Wolf family. From an early age, he was taught to hunt and kill small prey. The smaller and more vulnerable the prey the better and Mr and Mrs Wolf would encourage increasingly more painful deaths of anything hunted before they feasted. The Wolf was taught to become the ultimate hunter; stealthy and conniving, cold-blooded and unfeeling. As he observed his parents, the Wolf honed his skills and perfected his dark arts. He was rotten to the core and lived an angry existence. So much so that it was surprising he ever managed to convince another creature to bear his children. He had three children. His partner went missing mysteriously soon after they were born, amid rumours that the Wolf himself killed her once she had served her purpose. The Wolf raised them with as much love and hatred as his parents had raised him. However, the fact that he was on his own made things far more difficult and he was unable to continue the trail of evil that ran in the bloodline of the family. So much did the Wolf enjoy the hunt and the kill himself, he spent little time teaching his children; instead he would provide for them large banquets of venison, lamb, pork and beef. His children grew dependent on their father and they grew up to have no hunting skills whatsoever. They spent their lives moping around their den, waiting for their next meal to be brought to them. And the more they ate, the more the Wolf hunted and provided. The Wolf didn't care – he loved killing more than anything, even his own children, and the fact that he was feeding his family allowed him to justify his malicious actions to himself.*

After a long night of torturous killing and unnecessary

murdering, the Wolf was returning home, laden with heaps of dead meat, which he carried on his back. The number of animals he had killed that night went into double figures, although he only brought with him the finest cuts, the juiciest and most tender meats. He had expertly skinned and trimmed the carcases of each and every kill – the Wolf was extremely knowledgeable about which parts of an animal tasted best or were most rewarding in terms of nutritious content. Even though his children were lazy and overweight, he made sure that they still ate like kings. He entered his den expecting to hear the usual enthused greetings from the expectant brats – whoops of "Daddy's home!" or "Food's up lads!" or even "At last! I'm starving!" only on this occasion, there was a loud silence. There was nobody happy to see him come home and there were no shouts of celebration upon his arrival. He dumped his kills on the floor and anxiously called out for his boys. More silence. He frantically searched the den, knowing something was wrong. They never left the safety of home. They never had any reason or desire to do so. There were few who even knew they existed. The wolf had become so dominant, such an apex predator and this arrogance was likely to be his only weakness. So confident he had become, that he had grown sloppy and careless, underestimating those that despised him so.

The Wolf wondered. Not in a million years would anyone dare to venture near his den, let alone inside it. He began running through his mind the long list of names of those he had wronged over the years. But straight away he realised that that list was too long. So *he started thinking of the level of wrongdoing. Who had he upset most or to which animal, or human for that matter, had he done such terrible things that would have enraged them so much as to lead them to his den with revenge in mind. But once again, that list was also far too long. He would have been there for ages going through the different scenarios or remembering all the wonderful evil he had managed to act out. As much he liked to do that, now was not the time and the Wolf sat in the darkest and deepest corner of his hovel and changed his approach. He spoke to himself out load, his gravelly and gruff voice adding some comfort to him in the silence.*

"They didn't leave by choice. They never have. Someone's been here and someone's taken them. And I'm glad they did. Because when I find who did this, I'll have so much fun exacting my revenge. Whoever has been here and taken my children will wish they'd never been born. This will be your finest moment yet Wolf. This will act as a message to the rest of the world. I'll make such an example out of them." The Wolf took a thick steak of bloody venison and chewed at it, tearing and ripping at it and swallowing large chunks down in loud gulps. "So not who have I upset. Instead I must think who is capable of this. Humans yes. So many landowners and farmers I have aggrieved. But humans are simple creatures. For them it would not be personal and I would be dead – shot or left to die in a trap. No, not humans."

The Wolf's head rose, slowly. His eyes narrowed. From his slouched seated position on the floor, he got up and sauntered over to the entrance of his cave. Out into the mid-morning glare he walked. From where he stood, he had a panoramic view of Wakeman's Hill and the valley below. From there, the Wolf let out a long and deafening call.

"Pig!" he bellowed. His scream tore through the tranquillity of the day. Undergrowth rustled as animals ran for cover. Trees rushed and swished as birds flew out through the branches and up into the sky. Nature had answered the Wolf's cry. But it was up to him to find his children and seek the revenge he so yearningly desired. Of course, the pig to which Wolf referred was Jeremy. Only Jeremy had spent years of his life as a recluse. Only Jeremy would be capable of such a daring stunt. Only Jeremy would have found himself with so little to live for and so little to lose that going up against the Wolf would seem thinkable. It all started to become clear in the Wolf's mind. The three pigs. Had he underestimated them? As he toyed with them just days before when he stole their satchels while they slept, perhaps he hadn't joined the dots together as well as he might have. With his cry still echoing around the valley, the Wolf continued to ponder the next move and analyse events gone by. If the pigs managed to find the location of their distant father, they would have undoubtedly all rejoiced. The little time they'd spent together since would be more than enough for Jeremy to realise what he now had. The great pig's life now had meaning; he had something to live for. Something to fight for. Something to die for. This was an altogether different proposition. Any creature who has suffered loss of some kind has the right to be irked in some way. The type of loss and the reasons for the loss would also contribute to the levels of irk experienced. Wolf knew that Jeremy would have spent many months worrying and thinking what might have been. He knew that the pig would have built up a great deal of negative emotion. The three pigs would have told him everything. Prior to their arrival, Jeremy would have been hurting enough. Over four long years of pain and suffering, loneliness and solitude. Some of that pain might even have been lost to memory. If you think about something long enough, eventually you'll think it to be true. But those little pigs had changed everything. Those meddling runts. To describe Jeremy's likely response as outraged and incensed would not do it justice. Jeremy was a ticking time bomb and his children had just lit the fuse.

The Wolf gazed out across the valley and snorted with contempt. He was the king of everything he now looked upon. A mere pig was not going to make the slightest bit of difference. Standing on his hind legs, he stretched up and reached out his arms, straining and readying himself for the day ahead. He knew that this day would be quite unlike any other he had faced in a long time. He stood still for a moment, appreciating the calmness around him. The trees were still; the whole area seemed silent. A solitary bird swished its wings and twitched in a treetop, attracting the Wolf's attention. He drooped his head low and sniffed the ground, much in the same way Ron the farm dog had done near the beginning of this tale. Wolf's movements had suddenly become move reactive, more urgent. He prowled the stage that overlooked

Wakeman's Hill and with his head now high in the air, he inhaled all the scents around him. His breath became erratic; short, quick sniffs one second, followed long and deep gulps of air the next. Back and forth he strode, incessant, almost mesmeric, the way he paced about, revisiting sections he'd just been to, double and triple checking. His children were nearby; he could feel it. They were his reason to live; he existed for them. They were his reason to kill. He existed to kill. Without them, he was obsolete. Perhaps he was beginning to realise this. Perhaps Wolf now understood just how important his children were to him. They gave him the incentive and the motivation to keep on doing what he loved best. Yes, without them he'd still kill and kill frequently. But killing for them was far better than killing for the sake of killing. He'd spent years slaughtering animals (and the occasional lost human) for no reason and he enjoyed the fresh desire he now felt, every time he approached a new prey. A measly pig and his three useless sons were simply that; new prey.

For the umpteenth time, Wolf paced the walkway near the entrance to his cave. He slowed right down and began to take more precise sniffs, searching and being extremely particular about what and when he sniffed. He closed his eyes and crouched slightly, with his front legs out in front and his tail end raised. His large nose, moist with anticipation, rested on the ground between his front paws. In one fluid motion, he transferred his weight from his back legs to his front legs. The front of his body rose and took an enormous lungful of air in through his nose. He completed his inhalation just as his head reached its highest point. He stood tall, his back arched, his eyes still closed. And there he remained, perfectly still, listening to his nose. Wolf's eyes opened gently. He had it. The scent he'd been searching for. Pig. Or piglet. Whatever. It wasn't a strong aroma, just enough for the Wolf to pick out among all the traces of the morning. The sunrise dew had lifted and the air was clear. Now that he had the scent, Wolf knew he wouldn't lose it; it was just a matter of time before he discovered the pigs and rescued his children.

Learning more about their whereabouts with every whiff and with every step, the Wolf had time to think about what he might be presented with once he found them. Because he would find them, of that there was no doubt. But what did the pigs want with his kids? Was this a trick or was there something more sinister at play? Had the pigs kidnapped them to use as bait for the Wolf, or had the Wolf's actions driven them to contemplate something more worrying? Through the undergrowth he continued, taking the most direct route possible. He never was one for following the path and although this made his progress more difficult, it certainly enabled him to maintain his focus on the scent he was following. As soon as he sensed it getting weaker, he would pause and search, sniffing and scratching at the earth. The moment the scent became stronger, Wolf would stride purposefully over, under or through any obstacle in his way. His presence in the woodland was immense and other animals, petrified of his reputation more than anything else, would scarper immediately upon detecting his company. Most animals that didn't weren't alive to tell the tale – only their remains, or what was left of them, would act as an indication of their fate. Today, however, even though they wouldn't have known it, all the animals were safe. Wolf could come across a young litter of fox cubs on this particular morning and he wouldn't give them a second glance. He was fixated on one thing. Every deep, loud thud of his huge paws would resonate around the silence of the undergrowth; his usual stealthy prowl was of no use to him. The pigs knew he was coming for them; there was no need to be discreet.

Knowing the area as well as he did, Wolf felt he had an advantage, although he was perplexed as to where the scent of his children was leading him. And the scent was now stronger than it had been. Wolf knew he was close. He could hear the running water of the nearby river, which meant he was near cliff edge on the opposite side of Wakeman's Hill where the piglets had camped the night he stole their satchels. Soon, he'd reach the edge of the woodland altogether and be faced with the sheer drops he was familiar with. So many times before, he'd tormented his prey, pursuing them and almost herding them towards that edge, giving them the option of jumping to their certain death. Only this time, Wolf had no prey in his sights, just the smell of his stricken children in his snout. Sunlight began to creep through the darkened wood as the verge of the trees approached and the density of the leaves began to thin. Aware that he could be walking straight into a trap, Wolf stopped. Salivating, he took in his surroundings with keen senses, eyeing and sniffing at the slightest movement. For a long minute, he stood there, breathing calmly and holding his breath for elongated periods of time to enable him to really listen. A rustle to his left and the Wolf jerked his whole body round, instantaneously assuming an aggressive, powerful, crouching position. A sleepy squirrel, possibly roused from his slumber by the sheer tension in the woods, scampered wildly out of the darkness and darted past the Wolf. As quick as a squirrel trying to escape a large predator such as a wolf, the squirrel was gone in a flash and Wolf was once again alone, the only difference being a louder and more rapid breathing reverberating around the coppices.

With an almost nonchalant roll of the eyes, Wolf turned again to face the patchy openings at the edge of the wood, focused once more on his young family. To Wolf's right, a large shadow seemed to loom. It wasn't moving but Wolf definitely sensed an ominous darkness of some kind. He didn't move. He looked straight ahead, almost not wanting to let on that he'd sensed it. It was little wonder that the squirrel hadn't been able to sleep. The air was thick with an atmosphere. So still, yet electric. For another long moment, Wolf stood frozen, rooted to the spot. The leaves seemed to be watching, hanging from their branches like an audience, captivated by the theatrics below them. Not one of them dared move. Slowly, ever so slowly, the Wolf started to turn his huge head towards his right shoulder. Almost at the pace a flower might follow the sun through the day, it was difficult to actually observe the head turning but with each second that past, it was clear that Wolf had marginally moved. As the sinews in his powerful jaw tightened and the beginnings of a snarl began to form across his mouth, a long, heavy drool of saliva dangled from the Wolf's lower lip and released, falling onto the dusty floor.

And then their eyes met. Furrowed brows sat above dark pockets, which encased eyes that were full of emotion. All four of them. Anger, rage, dread, hatred; it was impossible to pinpoint exactly what either pair of eyes was saying. No words were necessary. No introductions were needed. Why waste energy on talking when you know you're about to engage in the fight of your life? The stare that each beast gave off could have pierced steel. Wolf displayed two extremes of nature's spectrum. As ugly and grotesque a beast as he was, Wolf was as impressive and as beautiful in equal measure. So powerful yet graceful. So bulky yet nimble. He was full of contradictions. Jeremy's awesome mass, on the other hand, was something to behold. Tough and rugged, he was a fearsome sight and his years out in the wilderness had made him unlike any pig seen anywhere. His dark years, spent suffering in the company of only his thoughts, had turned him into an unbreakable force; an immoveable object. And today these two forces stood opposite each other.

Although neither of them moved an inch, the energy that bounced around the leafy arena was alive. One could almost see it in the air, like heat rising in the desert. There was a coldness in Jeremy's face, the likes of which Wolf had never seen before; so blank and emotionless. The eyes said all that needed to be said.

They stared deep into the soul of the hunched Wolf and made him feel ever so slightly uneasy. Quick thoughts suddenly started jumping into Wolf's mind. His past, his parents, his children, his dastardly deeds, his victims. His future. He focused again but it was almost as though Jeremy had seen the process unfold in Wolf's own eyes. The faintest of smiles in the corner of Jeremy's mouth brought about an enormous rage in the guts of the Wolf. This rage rose up through his chest and burst into the throat of the great, vile beast. A terrifying roar erupted from the depths of the Wolf's body and exploded out into the air. A horrible noise, never before heard in the woods of Wakeman's Hill, rang out around the mountainside. The few birds, mammals or insects that remained in the enclosure fled in horror and the Wolf dug his claws into the dirt and leapt forward through the air towards the waiting pig.

Jeremy didn't flinch at the Wolf's scream; in fact, it appeared to comfort him. Any indication that Wolf was angry or displeasured was good news for Jeremy. Wolf had spent his whole hunting life as the predator; he didn't know what it was like to be prey. Wolf was in unfamiliar territory and he didn't even know it. Jeremy knew it. He could read the signs in Wolf's body language, in his behaviour. Besides, if Wolf had ever roared like that before, Jeremy would have known about it. The whole world may have heard that roar. As wolf flew through the air, Jeremy readied himself, planting his huge trotters firmly into the ground. Closer the Wolf came, eyes wide, teeth gnashing and slobber flying from his mouth due to the exertion of the leap. Wolf's hind legs bent into his stomach and his body twisted in the air. His right claw flew up above his head and razor sharp claws extended out, like five hooked knives. It was a bold and aggressive strike; a strike of anger and frenzy that lacked the usual control with which Wolf killed. It was a strike that left him vulnerable and Jeremy was not about to show mercy of any kind. The pig, who had only just managed to prevent his emotions from boiling over himself, swung a huge right fist towards the throat of the flying Wolf. Jeremy was well aware of the dangers and although he connected perfectly with his strike, the momentum that Wolf's attack had built up could not be slowed completely and those huge claws managed to find their way into his meaty shoulder. The power of Jeremy's blow caused Wolf to flip head over heels two, maybe three times and he bounced onto the dirt in a crumpled heap, coughing and spluttering, winded and shell-shocked. Jeremy winced as blood began to pour from the four large rakes across his left shoulder. Not willing to give the Wolf a moment to think, Jeremy sprang forward and the two beasts tumbled and tangled with each other, a great cloud of dead leaves and dust enveloping them as they fought. Biting and punching, pushing and tugging, they wrestled with each other, violent blows raining down, chaos ensuing. Indistinguishable screeches of fury and cries of pain resounded from the tumbling mass and the captivated leaves that looked on could not make out who was who, or what was what.

From up above, among the leafy spectators, there were also other members of the audience that had ringside seats. Three little pigs watched the unfolding massacre before them, as determined and angry as their own father below. Each of them held tightly onto the flabby neck of a terrified wolf cub. The helpless cubs had been tied so tightly that they couldn't move even to wriggle, and gagged so smartly that the only noise to escape them were the nearly silent hisses of their panicked breathing. All six of them were able to see their parents battling each other and they were all aware of the possibility that one of their fathers might be killed at any moment. The pigs hadn't taken the time or consideration to explain to the wolf cubs what was happening or why they had been kidnapped. Although it was very likely that they had a good idea what was going on. Wolf was known to be very boastful of his conquests and he liked spreading the rumours of his killing sprees and other dishonourable exploits. It was inevitable that on countless occasions over dinner, Wolf would have told and retold his wolf cubs the stories of his visits to Hillside Farm and his tormenting of Cynthia and Jeremy. These little useless good-for-nothings that now hung from the branches of the most dominant tree within the enclosure, were hated and despised by the three pigs as much as the Wolf himself. They knew what was happening. They understood the seriousness of their situation. What they didn't know was what was going to happen next. If the large pig below fell at the hands of their father, then the three pigs could easily snap their little necks – after all, what would they have to lose? But what if it was their own father, the terrifying Wolf himself who was slain before them? What would the pigs have in store for them then? Either way, it didn't look good for the wolf cubs.

The furore below came to an abrupt halt as the two foes parted from each other's grasps and rolled away. Once again they stood facing each other, exhausted and panting heavily, glaring towards one another. Both had sustained cuts and bruises. Each of the foes had delivered bone-crushing blows to each other. Yet there they stood, facing each other, chests heaving with each huge intake of breath. Jeremy was under no illusions as to the power and cunning of the Wolf. Wolf, however, was bewildered that a simple pig could withstand his terror. At one point during the almighty wrestle, Wolf thought he had surely won, when he sunk his huge jaws into Jeremy's shoulder, but so tough was the pigskin and so strong was the pig, that Wolf's bite barely registered a mark. More of a nibble than a bite. Befuddled and blinking, Wolf's demeanour was different. He no longer strutted around the arena confidently; it no longer felt like his arena. He suddenly became aware of the pain that soared through his entire body. Although the pig had not cut him, Wolf was in agony. Each heavy strike he'd received had done its own damage. Wolf's body throbbed. His ribs felt battered and his back felt as if an overwhelming force had crushed it. It hurt to breathe; a result of the devastating punch he received during his first attack on the pig. It was that strike that had done the damage. Wolf didn't realise it at the time but it had left him fighting for air and therefore unable to attack with his usual ferocity.

Without a moment's hesitation, Jeremy advanced fearlessly on the Wolf, forcing him closer to the cliff edge. Wolf attempted a low swipe with his left, which Jeremy kicked away with a meaty foot, jolting Wolf backwards again. For the first time, Wolf experienced the sensation of fear as he looked up at Jeremy and realised the relentless determination in his eyes. Wolf had never seen eyes like them. Calm and cold, full of hatred yet focused all at once. Jeremy towered over Wolf as he brought his trotters up above his head. Wolf raised his arms in an attempt to protect himself but to no avail. With earth-shattering force, Jeremy brought his fists down upon the traumatised Wolf, connecting with a sickening thud across the Wolf's head and neck. A wretched yelp rang out around the on-looking trees and the Wolf fell in a crumpled heap, breathing erratically and staring up at Jeremy with desperate eyes. His body was broken and his reputation was left in tatters. The legendary Wolf had been struck down in the prime of his life by a pig; an animal that he would usually destroy with one careless slap.

Davey, Harvey and Stanley climbed down from their viewpoint, each still clutching onto the stricken wolf cubs. They lay them down in front of the Wolf, as if to punish him further for the long history of upheaval he had caused.

"Before we kill you Wolf, we shall let your cubs go." spoke Jeremy, softly. "They will confirm to everyone what happened here today. The terror that you and your predecessors have inflicted on this countryside is over.

Your cubs will grow up feeble and lost, and with today's events clear in their minds forever." He approached the Wolf slowly, not out of fear that the beast might have one last attack in mind, but because he wanted to make this moment last. He felt all those years of solitude and hurt being washed away as he watched the Wolf twitching and convulsing on the floor before him. "Goodbye Wolf, and good riddance!" As he had done before, Jeremy raised his arms in the air, his piglets watching in awe and the tied up and gagged little wolf cubs followed him with wide eyes. He let out a tremendous roar, one the Wolf himself would have been proud of, and hammered his fists down onto where the Wolf lay.

But he was gone. It was as if the roar of the pig had woken the Wolf up just enough to give him the will he needed to lift himself up off the ground and jump. Off the edge of the cliff he'd gone. Jeremy looked at the two huge indentations his fists had left and for a moment, he could not understand what had happened. Stanley rushed past his father and was joined at the verge of the cliff by his brothers. All they could see was a cloud of dust leading all the way down to the river bank and the gentle ripples of the water as the current flowed downstream. For a long minute they stood there, desperately trying to find some evidence of the Wolf's demise. Or something to suggest that he had survived that awful drop. But there was nothing. The Wolf was gone.

Returning home

Jeremy took out the note that Henry had given to him. After releasing the wolf cubs into the wild and beginning their trek home, the piglets had seemed to lighten up a bit and were playing in and amongst the brushes and hedgerows up ahead. Jeremy read the note, the contents of which shall remain secret forever, but it is fair to say that he walked home tall and proud and with a strut in his step unlike any step he'd taken before. Henry, who had obviously been sent back by Cynthia to continue his reconnaissance missions, flew above their heads, occasionally swooping down and tagging the piglets with his wings. They would swipe at the homing pigeon as he plunged but they never even came close to catching him.

The greeting they received upon returning was memorable. Ron was standing at the gate, wagging his tail furiously. He was angry that the piglets had managed to sneak away without him realising but his delight that they were back safe and sound shone through with each flick of his tail. The adventurers were bundled into the farm without George the Farmer noticing and they made it to the pigsty, the entrance to which was barely recognisable, certainly to Jeremy who hadn't seen it in years. A party of epic proportions was held in their honour with not one Wolf in sight. Billy and Johnny had worked tirelessly to gather the animals together and organise the preparations. A feast the likes of which Hillside Farm had never seen before had been arranged, along with some games for the younger animals. They had even found time to put up some bunting and other decorations. It lasted all day and everyone was sent home by Claire at a reasonable hour, not that anyone could have partied for much longer, as exhausted as they were. The piglets were amazed at the transformation of their home and were particularly pleased with how comfortable their new beds were. Jeremy and Cynthia spent hours reigniting old flames, reminiscing about good times and planning their new future together. They were like teenagers in love for the first time once again; blushing and talking over each other, laughing and crying all at the same time.

The next day, Jeremy and his family woke up to a beautiful sunrise and walked out of their sty to find George standing there with one hand on his hip and the other scratching his beard. He looked at Jeremy as the huge pig strolled out into the morning sunlight. The farmer looked bemused and bewildered.

"Welcome home, I suppose!" George said, with a shrug of his shoulders. He slapped Jeremy on his shoulder as the pig eased past him and he could have sworn to himself that the pig seemed to grimace a little as he did so. There were plenty of scraps and leftovers waiting for the pigs to devour and Jeremy and his family wasted no time in chomping and munching their way through the entire pile with more gusto than George had ever seen during his many years as a farmer. Pigs are an essential aspect for the running of a farm and George was pleased that his prize pig was back and seemingly in better shape than ever. He had noticed in recent years that the quality of his manure had declined. Jeremy's return gave George a renewed excitement that this year's batch might be of the highest standard.

Later that day, Jeremy went for a walk around the farm to take in his surroundings once more. He visited Claire first and spoke with her at length about goings on at Hillside Farm during his years away. He expressed his deepest gratitude for her help and the two of them spent a moment together contemplating the past and thinking about how nice it was to have everyone back together. Next, Jeremy walked around Claire's field and, on his way back to the pigsty, he popped in to see Billy the Goat and Johnny the Cock, both of whom were delighted that he was back. Henry swooped down and listened intently as Jeremy told stories of his survival and turmoil. Billy and Johnny, who had always seen Jeremy as the father figure on the farm, looked up in awe at the huge beast and, as he walked away, they confirmed to each other that Jeremy had now been promoted to legendary or hero status in their opinion. Ron, the farm dog, had been sniffing around Jeremy for most of his stroll and had been eavesdropping throughout his visits to the other characters on the farmstead.

"Great to have you back, Jeremy." he said, proudly. "It's been rubbish around the farm without you here to keep everyone in check."

"Well, I've got no plans to leave again for a long while." Jeremy replied. "You can count on that." He gazed around his farm once more and noticed that Harvey, Davey and Stanley were playing in the mud pit outside their home. It was a sight that made Jeremy smile to himself. He was glad to be back; glad to be reunited with his family and glad to be wanted and needed and valued once more. The sun had begun to set and a gentle glow of warm red enveloped the farm. Jeremy took in a deep breath through his huge snout and smelt the air. Whiffs of the farm – food cooking in the farmhouse, manure steaming in the fields and the general stench that animals had about them, drifted through the air. And there was another smell. As Jeremy glanced past the exterior fence, he saw something glistening and flickering in the bushes. He gasped and for a moment his heart stopped beating. Jeremy squinted and watched but saw nothing more of it and turned to complete his circling of the farm, heading down to join his children in the mud pit.

Moments later, a twinkling eye blinked slowly from the bushes and a large dark shadow emerged, before skulking silently away into the night.

Author's note

My hope is to write more about the adventures of the three pigs and the other animals of Hillside Farm. I'd love to hear about what you thought of my book.

Please email me on philipmaddock@hotmail.com with your thoughts.

Thanks to Emma for all her support during the writing of this adventure. And to all of those who had some part to play in proof reading and sharing their ideas and opinions, all of which were gratefully received.

Printed in Great Britain
by Amazon